FOREWC

The pioneering work by the Seventh Earl of Shaftesbury, Anthony Ashley Cooper, in tackling Victorian child poverty through the work of the Ragged School Union is vividly portrayed in Norman Cook's novel. An exciting adventure story for children over the age of nine, this book should also be welcomed by parents and teachers alike. It provides an accessible insight into a historical period in which Britain was the 'workshop of the world', highlighting the contrasting effects of the industrial revolution upon the people of the day. The significant role of the Ragged School movement in response to those most poor and vulnerable is illustrated. Also, the strong motivation to make a practical difference is featured. Both these aspects still characterize the Shaftesbury Society today.

Fran Beckett
Former Chief Executive
The Shaftesbury Society (once the Ragged School Union)

Sam and the Glass Palace

Norman Cook

'You don't ketch me putting my money
into any o' them banks, I can tell yer!'

© Day One Publications 2005

British Library Cataloguing in Publication Data available.
ISBN: 1 903087 42 2

Published by Day One Publications
Ryelands Road, Leominster HR6 8NZ
Tel: 01568 613 740
Fax: 01568 611 473
email: sales@dayone.co.uk
web: www.dayone.co.uk

Design: Wild Associates Ltd
Tel: 0208 715 9224
Illustration: Gill Wild

CONTENTS

5

Norman Cook lives in Essex and was a Physics further education lecturer, for thirty-five years, before retiring in 2003. He has written a number of physics and engineering textbooks. Since retirement he has taught part-time at a university. In the early 1980s, while attending a Shaftesbury Mission, he wrote a number of plays on Christian themes. The first of these, a short drama called 'John Pounds, Ragged School Pioneer', inspired him to write a full-length musical, 'The Shaftesbury Story', on the career of the seventh Earl of Shaftesbury. Since then he has had an ambition to bring the work of Shaftesbury to a wider public.

Thanks are due to my wife, Brenda, also to Sian Brunton and Doug Crook for all the help and encouragement they gave me.

Chapter 1
ON THE STREETS

The short January day was marked by an icy wind blowing straight across the Thames. Scurrying from its chilling fingers, a slightly built boy about ten years old pulled his ragged coat around him and hunched his neck deeper into the threadbare collar. His pale face showed desperation and his stomach was hurting. He hadn't eaten for two days and even his last meal had been nothing but a few scraps of meat thrown out from the back of a soup kitchen and snatched before a hungry dog could pounce.

The streets of London in the harsh winter of 1850 were no place for an orphaned boy, but Sam Clarke had no choice. His father had taken to drink and lost his job as a locksmith. The only income was from Sam's mother's job as a sempstress, and worn out from hard work and too little food, she'd died two years ago. His father was incapable of caring for him; with drink inside him he couldn't even care for himself. One arctic night, just before Christmas, his body had been found in the backyard of their tiny house in Greenwich. He had returned home drunk and so helpless he couldn't get the door open and had frozen to death before morning.

Walking through the City's bustling alleyways, Sam staved off the pangs of hunger with fond memories of his mother and home. After supper at bed-time she would tell him stories before he went to sleep. His bedroom overlooked the river, where he used to watch barges, tugs and other river traffic go by. What he recalled most vividly was the first time he saw the steamer with its clunking paddles, so noisy that it almost seemed to be in their front room.

'It's the *Leith*, Sam, down from Edinburgh,' said his mother.

In common with most of the neighbourhood children he had rushed into the street and along the towpath, his arms flailing like paddles, imitating the high pitched hooting of the ship's siren. Some of the passengers began to wave at the crowd of onlookers and the excited children waved back. Sam noticed that the Leith had sails like most of the other ships but they were kept furled, only to be used in emergencies.

In a few minutes he was clear of the alleyways and turned into Cheapside from where he could see the vast bulk of St Paul's. Somehow it comforted him and reminded him of home. The better parts of the City always made him think of Greenwich, except it was all on a grander scale, of course. Soon he was in Pudding Lane and Sam could smell the hot bread from the shop on the next corner.

Now he had to be careful. On a previous occasion the baker's wife had taken pity on him when she found him with his nose pressed to the window, and slipped a small loaf into his pocket. She was a warm and friendly woman but her husband was a different matter. The sight of an urchin anywhere near the shop doorway would send him rampaging out with a large stirring spoon in his hand. Today Sam's luck was in. The woman was behind the counter and the baker was nowhere to be seen. She looked up, smiled in recognition and then beckoned him in. Sam smiled back. He sensed that she liked him. No one had taken a genuine interest in him since his mother died.

'You're looking hungry, boy. Haven't eaten for a good while, I'll be bound. How'd you like one of my specials?' She reached behind the counter and handed Sam a pork pie. It was freshly cooked and smelt delicious, and even better, it was hot enough to warm his frozen hands by.

'And put that away for later.' The woman pushed a package into his jacket pocket and then patted him tenderly on the cheek. 'If you don't mind waiting a bit, I think I've got some stale buns out the back.' Before Sam could thank her she swept into the back of the shop leaving him eating his pie by the counter.

A shadow fell across him and Sam glanced up. It was the baker returning to the shop and from the look on his face the boy sensed trouble. He knew he looked guilty and there was no time to explain as the man reached out towards him. The boy had been too long on the streets to be caught easily. He slipped under the baker's outstretched hand and bolted into the street.

'Stop thief,' came the cry and Sam ran even faster. He turned and the baker was in the street, pointing at Sam and shouting. One or two passers-by joined in, yelling and waving their hands and running after him. He heard their footsteps behind; it was time to act quickly. There was talk on the streets of an eight-year-old boy who had been sentenced to a month in prison and a whipping by the Clerkenwell magistrate, just for stealing boxes.

The river was his best hope; he had always lived near it and it made him feel secure. Soon he was by Billingsgate, the big fish market, vaulting over the wall on to the soft Thames mud below. Nearby was a large sewer opening, big enough for a boy to stand in. Sam slipped inside, paused long enough to make sure he wasn't followed and began to eat his pie ravenously.

The day after his father died, Sam remembered walking the streets in tears. He was on his own with no one to care for him. There was an uncle, his father's brother, but he was the leader of a gang of thieves that plagued the area south of the river and he ignored Sam completely. One night Sam met a ragged boy about his own age, who found him a barrel to sleep in near to the street market.

The boy knew some of the costermongers, the traders who sold fruit in the market, and one or two of the generous ones slipped them scraps to keep them going. When there was no market, the boy taught Sam to beg. They would stand, cap in hand, on street corners, asking for money. Sam hated doing it and sometimes he used to cry but he had no choice. Hunger drove him on. And it was risky too; the Peelers were always ready to arrest beggars and he didn't want a spell in prison or even transportation to Australia. Then there were the criminal gangs who would kidnap boys to beg for them and then keep all their takings. Strong and agile lads would sometimes be sold to chimney sweeps and then there was no escape. Sam had heard stories of climbing boys getting caught in chimneys and suffocating.

A passing tramp told them about London and how it was easy to live there, so they walked the few miles to London Bridge and crossed the Thames. A week later the other boy disappeared and Sam was left alone. Sam was worried for a time and asked some urchins if they had seen him.

'No, son we ain't seen no one but I expect one of the gangs 'ave 'ad 'im. If I was you I wouldn't ask too many questions, neither.'

The boys were obviously scared, so Sam didn't push the point but they seemed friendly enough and it was they who showed him the best places for street boys to eat and sleep.

Sam had finished eating now and he realized it was quite dark. The Thames was obscured by a thick river-mist and he could feel it pricking at his nostrils. His toes were beginning to tingle with the chill of the night air. Time for home and perhaps some sleep, he thought. 'Home' was the dry arch under the bridge, and the ragged waif who was Sam Clarke left the sewer outlet and made his way there.

Most of the arches that made up the bridge were built over the river and the dry arches were those at the ends, built over the river banks. By the time he arrived some of the others were already back and were talking about the day they'd had. They'd been to the

Covent Garden Market and were boasting about their takings. Usually they went along in gangs and while one jostled a rich-looking gentleman in the crowd, another picked his pocket, removing money, snuff-boxes, watches – anything they could find. Two other boys would keep watch. Today they had found rich pickings, including ladies' jewellery, and were in high spirits. One of them had obtained a top hat from somewhere and he was prancing around with his nose in the air pretending to take snuff.

''Ere, ain't 'e the gent then, ain't 'e Lord Muck,' said another, clutching his stomach and roaring with laughter.

A third, wearing an expensive necklace and gold bracelets, tried to knock the top hat to the ground and the two rolled in the dust in a good-natured wrestling match. The rest stood around, alternately jeering and shouting encouragement.

Sam watched the proceedings with interest and amusement. He didn't agree with stealing; his mother had made him commit the Ten Commandments to memory. But some of the boys had a real talent for making people laugh and when they grew up, would probably make a living entertaining at one of the cheap taverns in the area.

The boys thought they were rich and would be swaggering about and boasting for the rest of the evening. Sam knew, though, that it would not last. First of all, adult vagrants who lived under the arch with the boys would want their share. Secondly, the boys themselves weren't too careful with their money. In a few days it would all be blown on beer, gin and whisky and then they would go out stealing again.

Later in the evening the grown-ups came back. Mostly they were men but there were women too. They usually spent their days either begging or slumped in doorways swigging liquor. Just as Sam expected they quickly discovered the boys' haul and divided most of it between them.

The night drew on, the mist grew thicker and the cold grew more intense. The company of arch dwellers, the men, the women, the boys and girls, huddled together under an old tarpaulin. Some of the men were drunk and trying to sing but the weather beat them. It was too cold for any kind of jollity.

Sam tried to sleep but it wasn't easy on the hard ground, and in any case he couldn't get really warm. He must have dropped into a slumber, however, because around midnight he was half awakened by a shout from one of the lookouts. Lookouts were those who slept at the outside edges of the sleeping group so they could warn of danger.

'Kool esclop,' came the cry again. Sam and the others were all wide awake by now. 'Kool esclop' was a warning given in backslang, a type of code used by London vagrants, traders and criminals to prevent outsiders from understanding what was said. All you had to do was to say each word backwards. 'Kool' meant look and 'esclop' was police so 'kool esclop' stood for 'look (out for) the police'. Yenep was a penny in backslang.

'It's the Peelers,' one of the men was yelling.

'Leave us alone, we ain't done nothing,' shouted another.

Sam heard rapid footsteps as most of his companions disappeared into the darkness but he, himself, did not move. After all, a night or two in the cells wasn't too bad; at least you had something to eat. In any case Sam had his doubts about the approaching group. Although cautious, he was a brave lad who refused to panic. He would only run if absolutely necessary. The boy sat up and listened. It didn't sound like the police. The footsteps were slow and measured, which suggested walking not running and the people were talking in normal conversational tones.

Perhaps it was charity workers from the London City Mission, he thought. Sometimes they came round and gave you food. Occasionally there was shelter for the night.

The lights of several torches flared in the darkness, along the path that led to the bridge. As they neared the sleepy forms under the arch, Sam saw a large party of well-dressed gentlemen. The leading figure was elderly with white hair and he was talking to a bearded, dark-haired, middle-aged man right behind him. The other children shrank back under their tarpaulin in case it was one of the gang leaders of the area, but Sam knew differently. The group reached the arch and stopped.

'How many boys and girls do we have here tonight?' asked the middle-aged man. He seemed very tall and stern but when he talked to the children he smiled in a way that Sam liked because it lit up his whole face, not only the mouth but the eyes as well.

'Come on now, I'm not going to hurt you, I'm trying to help. My name is Shaftesbury, the Earl of Shaftesbury. How many of you would like a hot drink and something to eat? And, if you want, after you've all eaten I'll find you a warm bed for the night.'

At the sound of the word 'eaten' the assembly of waifs leapt out from the tarpaulin and clustered around the speaker, shouting and cheering. The Earl quietened them and gave the order to follow him.

'Keep close to me or you may get lost; we've quite a walk in front of us.'

So with Shaftesbury in the lead, the ragged band following, and the Earl's helpers bringing up the rear, they set off towards food and shelter.

Chapter 2
THE RAGGED SCHOOL

The Earl had been right when he said the walk was a long one, and Sam felt tired by the time they arrived at an old factory building with a heavy wooden door. As Lord Shaftesbury produced a large key from his pocket to let them in, Sam heard a distant church clock strike one. The exhausted urchins filed into the gaslit hall and then stood bewildered at the vision before them. For right there in the room was a table groaning with food and drink; something none of them had seen before. Behind the table stood a number of churchy-looking ladies in flowered hats, ready to serve. And surprisingly, to those used to the hunted life of the streets, they were not angry but smiling and cheerful.

''Ere look at that, boys,' Sam heard one of his companions shout, 'I've never seen so much grub in all my life.'

The words began a stampede towards the food where the waifs began cramming handfuls of bread and cake into their mouths. A scrummage formed and a large jug of tea was knocked over.

'That's enough,' a voice shouted over the din. 'That's quite enough, I will not stand for that kind of behaviour in here.' Sam took a long look at the Earl as he tried to calm the young vagrants. Behind the stern exterior there seemed to lurk a great sadness, a sadness that showed in the eyes. It had been the same with his mother. There the inner unhappiness was untouched, even at family Christmases. The hubbub died and the ragged children shifted uneasily, then stood staring nervously at the commanding figure.

'Right! Now that's much better. You boys at the front, put that food down this instant and come to the back. The rest of you go to the table and form an orderly queue.' Not knowing quite what to make of the imposing stranger, the urchins mutely did as they were told.

A few minutes later, Sam and the others were sitting on benches with bowls of soup in their hands, eating hungrily. Sam had never seen his companions so subdued. As he ate, his eyes roamed the room, taking in his surroundings. High up on the walls were notices of some sort that the boy wished he could read.

From the time he was five until about a year before she had died, his mother had sent him to a dame school, where an old woman had attempted to teach hordes of local children. Discipline had been bad, and in any case his mother was too poor to send him every day, but still he had managed to learn a little. Sunday School had taught him a bit more but he wasn't yet capable of reading printed notices. As the waif sat there, his spirits lifted by the food before him, he resolved that if ever he got the chance he would make sense of those notices and learn to do everything that adults could do.

At the far end of the bare brick hall was an old fireplace and a grate where a bright coal fire burned. Sam could feel the heat and smell the smoke and he felt cheered. He hated the numbing cold of the streets. Above the fireplace was a picture of a man in eastern costume, standing by some sheep and Sam recognized him as Jesus. Scattered about the room in various corners were stools and benches clustered around blackboards.

It was obvious, if you looked closely, that the place had been a factory. There were dried patches of oil on the flagstones and a beam with machinery attached stuck out just below the ceiling. The walls were clean and fresh but painted by volunteers rather than experts, guessed Sam.

'Well, children, I trust that you're enjoying your meal.' It was Lord Shaftesbury again. This time there was a smile behind the beard.

'Some of you may be wondering why you are here,' he continued. 'The fact is this place is a school but it is a special one. As you know, in other schools, such as those run by the churches, your parents have to pay'. At that a murmur of protest went up from the assembly but the speaker silenced them by raising his hand.

'Yes, I know many of you don't have parents or else you have them but you no longer live with them and I'm truly sorry. But the fact is that nobody has to pay for this school; you can all come here for nothing. It is called a ragged school and I am speaking to you not as a lord but as the President of the Ragged School Union. You see we have many other schools similar to this, which, by the way, is called Field Lane Ragged School and we are at a place called Holborn.'

'If you want to attend here and learn your lessons, you are welcome. However, I cannot force you and you are free to leave whenever you please. If you want to sleep here because you have nowhere else, there is a night shelter at the back of the building. That is all I have to say for now, so I'll bid you good night and place you in the good hands of our headteacher, Mr White.'

Lord Shaftesbury took his top hat from the hook, shook Mr White's hand, waved to the children and was gone.

Mr White was a short, middle-aged man with just a wisp of hair brushed across the top of his head. 'If you'd all like to come along with me, I'll show you where to sleep,' he said. The raggle-taggle band was led to a room at the back of the hall, where the floor was covered in straw-filled mattresses.

'The boys can sleep in here and the three girls can have the small room under the stairs. I'll wake you in the morning and explain about the school.' Sam's eyes closed as soon as he lay down and he slept the sleep of exhaustion.

'Come on boys, it's half past eight. Time for a wash; you start school in an hour. When you've finished, report to me in the schoolroom.' Mr White led the still sleepy urchins into the washroom, where there were jugs of hot water and some bowls.

Sam groaned inwardly. The room was freezing, the floor was stone and he could feel an icy draught from under the door. Half an hour later the freshly scrubbed urchins, still smarting from their ordeal, presented themselves to the headteacher. The girls were already there, so Mr White began to explain the school's daily routine.

'I let you lie in this morning because you were late to bed but normally you'll be called at six and you're expected to sweep and clean the school before your morning wash. Then it's breakfast, usually bread with a mug of tea to drink and the school opens at nine.'

'Between nine and half past Miss Stretton or I read from the Scriptures. Miss Stretton is my assistant and she is in charge of the girls. Then we sing a hymn, say our prayers and we're ready to start.'

Sam saw some of the others exchanging glances and raising their eyebrows. He knew they were thinking the discipline was hard and they'd rather be free on the streets. But the streets weren't for him. He'd rather stay. Mr White, too, noticed the restlessness but he ignored it and continued speaking.

'From half past nine till eleven we have reading and spelling and then eleven to half past twelve it's arithmetic and writing. We have half an hour for dinner, usually bread and soup. Some of you might prefer to come here just for the food,' the headteacher smiled.

'Early in the afternoon we play games in the park and then when we come back it's time to learn a trade. The boys have a choice of tailoring or shoemaking and the girls can do sewing. At five o'clock it's tea time; you get a mug of tea and a slice of bread. Most of the day children go home to their families after tea but we have Scripture reading, singing and sometimes geography up to about eight o'clock.'

By the time Mr White finished, the school had started filling up with day children and teachers were arriving. A severe-looking woman with her hair tied in a bun (Sam assumed it was Miss Stretton) started playing the piano. Soon the children were learning the words of the Twenty-Third Psalm and attempting to sing it to Miss Stretton's music.

For the reading lesson Sam was placed with the other street boys to be taught by Mr White. The girls went with Miss Stretton. The headmaster wasted no time in getting started. He sat his charges on a bench in front of him and quickly cleaned the blackboard from the previous day.

'There are slates over there. Take one and a piece of chalk each.' The waifs did as they were told and sat waiting for the lesson to start.

'We'll begin with the alphabet, I'll write the letters on the board, then I'll say them and finally you say them with me. The first letter is called A.'

'A is for apple,' they chanted, after carefully trying to copy it on to their slates. Sam made several attempts and finally ended up getting the shape more or less right.

'A is for apple; B is for ball; C is for cake,' the lesson continued. When Mr White was satisfied enough of the alphabet had been covered and his pupils had at least a reasonable understanding, he brought out a pile of old books.

'These have been given to us by churches and other charitable institutions. I prefer them to new books because I can pull them apart and take out the pages I need. Mostly they are Bibles but there are some adventure books as well.'

The headmaster sorted carefully through the pile, pulling out loose pages here and there so that each boy had the reading material he could cope with. Sam's page had a picture on it of what looked like a giant tied down on a beach with tiny figures climbing all over him.

'Now I'll take you one at a time to see what your reading ability is like. You, the little boy at the front, what's your name?'

'It's Sam, sir.'

'Well, Sam, come here and I'll read your page to you. Then we'll see what you make of it. This is a book called *Gulliver's Travels* and the first few lines go like this.'

'My father had a small estate in Nottinghamshire; I was the third of five sons.' Now you try Sam. The first word is only short and quite easy, so try it for yourself.'

'My,' said Sam, uncertainly, 'F-A-T-H-E-R, fath, fath, father.' And so it went on with a lot of prompting from Mr White, especially over Nottinghamshire and a lot of guessing from Sam. Directly he could see the boy's attention beginning to wander he finished *Gulliver's Travels* at a suitable place and went on to the next pupil.

By the end of the lesson Mr White had read with every boy in the group. After a short break taken in the yard outside the school, it was time to learn some numbers. Mr White wrote them on the board and the pupils were made to copy them. From time to time they had to recite them until they knew them all by heart.

Soon it was lunch-time with oxtail soup. Afterwards they played cricket in the park.

In the afternoon, Sam chose shoemaking for his craft and made a start with a very sharp knife and a pile of leather. After tea there were more lessons and by the time evening hymn singing finished, an exhausted Sam flopped into bed.

The days and weeks sped by and Sam gradually got used to the daily routine. He noticed that many of those rescued from the dry arch had slipped away, never to be seen again. Probably they were back on the streets and sleeping rough once more. He also looked around him to see how the ragged school operated.

One thing he observed was that the standard of instruction varied a lot from teacher to teacher. They were all volunteers, most were keen and capable but some were very bad. The bad ones either could not keep discipline among the unruly street children or had little education themselves to pass on. The best of them, however, were very good indeed and one such was Miss Stretton.

She was an expert at finding things children were interested in and then using that interest to get them to learn. One day, during a lull in Sam's lesson, he began to notice the way that she dealt with her group. One of the girls was holding a yellow flower she had picked up somewhere outside.

'What's that you're holding in your hand, Polly?'

'It's a buttercup, Miss Stretton.'

'And how do you spell butter?'

'B-U-T-T-E-R.'

'Now spell cup.'

'K-U-P.'

'No, Polly, C-U-P. And is it a pretty flower?'

'Yes, very pretty.'

'Spell pretty.'

'P-R-E-T-T-Y.'

And so the lesson went on, not just with Polly but with others too, all given individual attention.

Polly was a pleasant, dark-haired girl who had started at Field Lane before Sam. The others said she was funny and good at doing impressions of adults, especially the teachers. But he had never spoken to her before, so during the morning break, he approached her and congratulated her on her reading.

'I wish I could read like you but no matter how hard I try, I don't seem to get anywhere,' said Sam.

'Nah, don't worry, you've only been here five minutes. You'll soon get the 'ang of it.'

Seeing that Polly was friendly, Sam started to tell her about his life before coming to the school. He unburdened himself at some length and then he became curious about her own background.

'What about you, Polly? How did you come to be here?'

'Well, Sam, it's a long story and a sad one too but no worse than yours. My mum and dad worked at Covent Garden in the fruit market or they was supposed to. The trouble is they never did nothing. Mum was always drunk and dad never got up in the mornings.'

'The only ones that did any work was me and my sister. We was both watercress girls. I did that from the time I was seven. You 'ad to get up at dawn with your basket and go down to Covent Garden to get your cress. Two shillings the old man used to give me to pay for it. 'E was too lazy to get up, so I 'ad to go and get the money from 'is pocket.'

'I expect you were tired out with all that work,' said Sam.

'Yeah, I was and they expected me to look after the 'ouse when I got in. Then when I got older, me and my sister 'ad to dance for the customers in a penny gaff.'

'I never heard of a penny gaff, Poll.'

'It's a place with a stage at the front. There's a band and singing and dancing. You 'ave singers and comics who tell jokes. It costs a penny to get in and then lots of the crowd get drunk and shout things out. And me and my sister 'ad to dance on the stage between all the other acts. We 'ated it; we used to cry ourselves to sleep at night. And my dad got all the money.'

'So what did you do? Did you run away?' said Sam.

'We talked about it but before we could do anything the neighbours complained about mum and dad being noisy and dirty and not looking after us properly, so the whole family got took to the workhouse. Me and my sister didn't like it, so this time we did run away and I ended up in the ragged school. The trouble is my sister ran the other way and I ain't seen 'er since.' A tear started to trickle down her cheek and she wiped it away with her sleeve.

'I'm sorry about your sister, Poll, but I'm glad you're here. I know,' said Sam suddenly grinning, 'I'll call you Dancing Poll.'

'I don't only dance, Sam,' said Poll and then she chuckled, 'Listen to this. I've been working on it. Perhaps I'll be back on the stage one day.'

Poll's shyness disappeared, her brown eyes flashed and suddenly she grinned from ear to ear. Then she started to pull a series of funny faces, each face going with an imitation of a teacher's voice. After a while they both laughed so much that they collapsed and rolled on the floor. In the next few weeks she established a firm reputation for her impressions throughout the school and would do them to order.

Sam worked very hard at his lessons and was soon known as the most ambitious pupil in the school. He was determined not to go back on the streets and so he learnt everything he could. He became particularly good at shoemaking and Mr White praised him for his skill.

Sam liked Mr White for a number of reasons. One was that it was obvious he wasn't comfortable in his high starched collar and three-piece suit. Another was that he did not speak with a really smart accent, like Lord Shaftesbury. The boy guessed that the headteacher's voice had originally been cockney like his own and that gave him hope. If Mr White could do it, then so could he.

Miss Stretton wasn't like Mr White. Sam liked her too but she spoke rather like a female Shaftesbury and he knew he could never be like that. She must be rich because he had seen her arrive at school on a coach, driven by a coachman. He found himself fascinated by the powerful smell of her perfume, her sparkling jewellery and by her coats, all with fur collars.

One day Mr White called Sam into his office. He had a letter in his hand and he looked very pleased.

'I've had a letter from Mr John Macgregor of the Ragged School Union. He wants a group of intelligent lads to train as shoeblacks. It's a marvellous opportunity, Sam, and I'd like you to try. You'd be cleaning gentlemen's shoes and getting paid for it. And more than that there's a special job that he wants you to do, though he doesn't say what it is. The only thing is you'll have to move away from here and live in Kensington.'

Sam looked crestfallen. 'Does that mean I won't go to school any more and I'll never learn to read? And what about my shoemaking?'

'No need to worry, we've got a school in Kensington and you'll go there in the afternoons after learning to clean shoes in the mornings. As for the shoemaking, you can always come back to that, at a later stage, after you've done this special work for Mr Macgregor. Think about it and let me know by tomorrow.'

'Mr Macgregor is a very clever man who is nearly as famous as

Lord Shaftesbury himself among the officers of the Ragged School Union. So this is a chance in a lifetime.'

By the next morning had made up his mind. He would be a shoeblack and earn himself some money. After all, what had he to lose? He would still be learning his lessons. At break-time he said goodbye to all his friends including Poll, whom he promised to visit on his free days. Kensington was too far for the boy to walk, so Mr White arranged for a local carter to take him there. Before Sam went, there was one thing he had to do. He went to look at the notices on the walls and this time he could read some of the shorter words. 'Thou' was one and 'not' was another. One day, thought Sam, I shall read them all.

Minutes later he was perched atop bulging potato sacks, stacked on a massive wooden cart, waving goodbye to his friends from Field Lane. The huge shire horse, like an elephant to the nervous boy, hauled the enormous load slowly away from the school and into the teeming streets of Holborn.

Chapter 3
ROB ROY

On Mr White's instructions the carter dropped Sam off at a tall, narrow building with a freshly painted notice indicating it was the Shoeblacks' Lodging. A bricked-up door, with a hoist above, opening out into empty space high up near the roof, told Sam it was a disused warehouse.

'Just go inside and ask for Mrs Clayton, then give her this letter,' said the carter, handing Sam an envelope.

Sam jumped down from his seat beside the driver and entered the hallway of the lodging house. The smell that greeted him was one he was familiar with but did not much like – carbolic soap. In the background was a faint odour of floor polish.

An elderly cleaning woman peered at Sam with ill-concealed dislike.

'Whatchoo doin' 'ere, I 'opes you ain't gonna cause no trouble. We don't want no young ruffians about the place. This is a respectable gaff.'

'Please, I think I'm going to stay here. I've got a letter for Mrs Clayton,' said Sam, not knowing what a ruffian was and afraid the woman might start shouting.

The old woman sighed and then noisily sucked in air through her front teeth, dimpling her cheeks as she did so. "Old on then, I'll fetch her, but it's more than my job's worth. I expects I'll be dismissed for this and end up in the workhouse.' She shuffled off down the dimly- lit corridor, sniffing and muttering to herself.

In a few minutes a stout, red-faced woman in a starched apron appeared. She, too, smelt of carbolic soap. 'Good morning and who are you?' said the woman. Her voice was polite but firm. Not the kind of person Sam wanted to argue with.

'Please, miss, I'm from Field Lane Ragged School and I've got a letter for you.' He handed it to the woman and as her eyes scanned the page Sam looked anxiously at her face. Perhaps she'd turn him down, so he'd have to go back to Field Lane in disgrace and never become a shoeblack.

The woman glanced up. She had finished reading.

'What's your name, lad?'

'Sam, miss.'

'Hello, Sam, and just one thing, I'm Mrs Clayton, not miss. Mr Clayton, the warden, is my husband and we run the place between us. Field Lane wants me to put you up while you train as a shoeblack and I'll be glad to do that. I've learnt to trust Mr White's judgement. He's never let me down with a boy, yet.' Sam gave a little sigh of relief. He'd been accepted.

'If you'll follow me, I'll show you your new lodging house.' Sam followed the woman as she indicated the various rooms.

'This is the dormitory where you'll be sleeping. I'm afraid we can't afford beds but all the mattresses you see on the floor are clean. There's twenty of you in here which is really too many. Mr Macgregor has put in for a bigger building but that will have to wait until the Ragged School Union can raise the money.' They walked down some stone stairs to the basement.

'The door in front of you is the washhouse and you must have a wash every day. Most of the boys don't like it much, so I'm always around first thing in the morning to make sure that everyone is clean.' Mrs Clayton smiled for the first time and Sam blushed. He had never liked washing when he lived at home and he had lost the habit completely living on the streets.

The woman seemed to know exactly how his mind worked. 'All this is very hard work for my staff. They have to bring all the water, cold and hot, in buckets from the kitchen,' the woman continued. 'So you might at least show your appreciation by washing properly. I've got worse news, still. The room next door has a bath and you must use it once a week. Friday night is bath night and it is even harder on the staff.'

Sam sighed. There had to be a catch in his good fortune somewhere, he thought. If there was one thing he hated more than washing, it was taking a bath. Mrs Clayton chuckled and gently ruffled his hair. 'Just look at those big blue eyes of yours and all that fair hair. You'll break a few hearts when you get older, I shouldn't wonder.'

The next room was large and furnished with wooden chairs and small tables. 'We call this the gymnasium and some of the boys come in to do exercises. It's also used for games like draughts and dominoes. If you can't play, I expect the others will teach you.'

Mrs Clayton completed the guided tour at the kitchen with its black-leaded ovens and scrubbed wooden cutting tables. Despite its cleanliness the room still smelt of boiled cabbage and custard. The pump in the corner was the only water supply for the entire building. Finally there was the dining room, equipped with heavy trestle tables and long benches.

'Well, that's it for the moment. If there's anything else I expect you'll find out soon enough. But I have to read a list of the charges we make and the rules you have to obey. We do that for every boy who comes here, so I might as well do that now.' She smiled, adjusted her bonnet and took down a dog-eared notice that hung from a nail in the entrance hall.

'Bed tuppence per night; pint of tea one penny; loaf of bread one penny; butter one penny; soup one penny and a large piece of cold meat a penny halfpenny. That's the food and we don't charge for cooking it. You'll have Sundays free and we do you a meat dinner at one o'clock. Any questions?' Mrs Clayton paused but Sam couldn't think of anything, so she continued.

'As far as the washhouse is concerned, looking glasses, towels and combs are provided.' She saw the corners of his mouth turn down and smiled to herself.

A tall man with a bushy beard and dark suit pushed through the door and after tossing his broad-brimmed hat on the hatstand he came over to join them. Mrs Clayton introduced him as her husband, the warden.

'Have you told him about the opening hours, my dear,' said Mr Clayton. 'He's got to know when he can come and go, otherwise he won't know where he is.'

'No need to worry, I was just coming to that.' Mrs Clayton frowned at the interruption and then continued. 'The lodging house opens at six in the morning and closes at ten o'clock of an evening. All candles must be out by half past and we want no noise or trouble during the night. Is that clear, Sam?' The boy nodded and the warden's wife continued.

'When you start as a shoeblack, you'll work mornings only and go to ragged school in the afternoon. When you get back here you give all the money you've earned to the warden or myself.'

'D-does that mean that I have to work and won't get any money for it?' said Sam in a disappointed voice.

'No, it doesn't, Sam,' said the warden. He had wandered off to talk to a group of boys who had come into the building but now he was back again. 'You get sixpence a day to buy dinner or you can give it to my wife and she'll pack you some food to take with you. That makes a total of three shillings a week, because you don't work on Sundays. Then from your earnings you get a shilling to spend on yourself. Another shilling goes into our Savings Bank and I write it all down in a big book. You get all that money back when you finally leave us. Lastly, any money left over helps to pay for things like new mattresses, Sunday dinners and general upkeep.'

The warden paused and Sam smiled politely but said nothing. He was unused to money of any sort and he certainly wasn't going to object to the terms set out by the tall, bearded man in front of him. He had been long enough on the streets to grow nervous of authority.

'Tom,' Mr Clayton called and a boy from the group joined them. 'I tell you what, Sam, I'll hand you over to Tom, here, he'll show you the ropes.'

Tom was a snub-nosed boy who was taller than Sam and looked a lot older. 'Come on, Sam, you come along with me and meet some of the boys. You can sleep on my side of the dormitory along with Charley and Bill. They're my mates. Anyway, there's plenty of time to sleep later, so we'll go to the gym.' Tom gave a broad grin and led the way.

The draughtsmen and dominoes were set out ready for a game and a group of boys sat at a table, laughing and joking with each other. Tom ignored them. 'That's what I like,' he said, pointing towards the ceiling. Sam looked up and saw a ladder fixed there. 'You can swing by your arms from one side of the room to the other,' said Tom. 'That is if you've got strong arms.' The boy shinned up the wall bars and pausing only to flex his muscles and grimace at the others, he made his way, at high speed, rung by rung, from one side of the ladder to the other. 'Now beat that!' he shouted as he vaulted cat-like to the floor.

Some of the others attempted to meet his challenge but all of them were forced either to drop before they got right across or else they succeeded but only with great difficulty.

Each time someone fell a great roar of laughter went up. 'Now it's my turn,' shouted Sam excitedly, determined not to be the odd one out and everyone stopped and stared. He gritted his teeth and gripped a rung with all his strength but the street life had left its mark. His arms just weren't strong enough and he tumbled straight to the ground. Some of the boys laughed but Tom glared fiercely, his fists clenched and his freckled face red with anger. Dark brown curls, normally brushed back, tumbled across his forehead. Tom wasn't a lad you tangled with if you could avoid it.

Tom helped Sam to his feet and took him to the dormitory where the badly shaken boy sat dejectedly on a mattress. Shortly after, they were joined by two boys Tom introduced as Charley and Bill.

'Don't worry young 'un. In a few weeks, with Mrs Clayton's food you'll be as strong as any of 'em. I'll make sure of that,' said Tom. 'By the way, are you coming with us tomorrow to meet Rob Roy?'

'Rob Roy, who's that?' said Sam, looking puzzled.

'He's the one who's teaching us to be shoeblacks,' said Bill. 'Mr Macgregor, he's Scottish and proud of it. And don't let him catch you calling him Rob Roy or you'll be for it.'

'But why Rob Roy?' said Sam.

'Rob Roy was some kind of outlaw, a kind of Robin Hood but Scottish and his name was Macgregor,' said Bill, the brainiest of Tom's friends.

That night Sam got little sleep, partly because he was so excited and partly because some of the boys talked, laughed and scuffled until the small hours of the morning. Eventually Tom, who was unofficial leader, managed to quieten them down. When Sam eventually fell into a slumber, he did so secure in the knowledge that, for the first time since his mother died, he had a friend and protector.

Early next morning, when breakfast was over, the lodging house boys set off for the ragged school, just a few streets away. It turned out to be a former chapel converted into a school building, the only school Sam ever went to that had stained-glass windows. The whole area was much smarter than that near the lodging house with its smoky atmosphere and barefoot children playing in the gutters.

Here the menfolk worked in clean new workshops producing high-quality goods for export throughout the Empire. Their children went to Church of England schools and their wives developed middle-class accents. The families were well dressed but you could tell they weren't toffs. Somehow they didn't walk in quite the right way and wore their hats at the wrong angle. In those days, when Britain was the workshop of the world, there were really two working classes: one an impoverished underclass and one which was quite well off and getting wealthier.

Mr Macgregor was different from most of the other ragged school masters. For one thing he dressed a lot smarter, with a suit that was always neatly pressed. His chin was clean shaven, he had no sideburns and unlike many Victorian men, he kept his hair short. He also had a trim moustache and spoke in a brogue that Sam later recognized as Scottish. His memory was bad and he called all his charges laddie, until he knew them well. When he made jokes, he usually didn't smile at all and you could only tell he was amused by the slight wrinkling of the skin round his eyes.

At the beginning of their first lesson on shoe cleaning, Rob Roy told his brigade of ragged boys something of the life of Lord Shaftesbury, President of the Ragged School Union.

'He came from a very wealthy family but his parents neglected him and took no notice of him at all. Instead, they left him in the hands of the housekeeper who happened to be a strict Christian woman. She alone loved him, looked after him and told him about God. It was her influence which gave Shaftesbury his burning sense of injustice and the desire to do something about it. When he grew up he became an evangelical Christian in the Church of England. He decided that his best way to serve the country was to become a Member of Parliament and right some of the wrongs he saw about him. He worked hard and managed to stop children being made to work long hours in factories. He also stopped women and children from working in filthy conditions in coal mines. And lastly, just to make you feel proud, Lord Shaftesbury works for many charities but his favourite is the Ragged School Union. He told me so himself.'

The former street urchins were worked hard by Mr Macgregor who always insisted that things were done properly. In just a few weeks they were taught to use their polishes, brushes and cloths to give dull shoes a bright shine.

When Sam first saw Rob Roy clean a pair of shoes, he found it difficult to believe how quickly and efficiently the job could be done by an expert. And what's more they seemed to fairly sparkle with the gloss he put on them. Now it was the turn of the boys and their leader refused to let up on them till, weeks later, they all did as well as he.

From time to time Mr MacGregor would illustrate some aspect of shoe cleaning by a Bible story. For example, he impressed on them the necessity for hard work by talking about the parable of the talents. In biblical times a talent was a coin and if you buried your talents and never used them, you would never prosper in whatever you attempted. Somehow, during his few weeks with the group the resourceful Scot managed to preach the gospel to them in such a way that they hardly knew they were being taught. He explained how Jesus had been crucified to save us all and how anyone could be saved by repenting of sin. Every day, before lessons, he prayed for his trainees as a group and then, if there was time, he knelt with each boy individually and prayed with him.

'Ye can pray for whatever ye really want most in the whole world,' the kindly Rob Roy said to Sam, when it was his turn. The young shoe black was nervous at first but deep down inside he knew what he wanted. So he shut his eyes, concentrated hard and simply said what had been on his mind ever since he had been orphaned.

'Please, God, send a mum and a dad to look after me and a home to live in.'

The Scot smiled and ruffled Sam's hair.

During the afternoon school sessions Sam continued to make progress and was able to read parts of quite difficult books. One day, during lesson time, he noticed a man with an artist's sketch pad sitting at the back of the hall. At break time he and his friends went to see the drawings. They were cartoons of children in the school, some attending to their lessons and others getting up to mischief. The whole group burst out laughing as they recognized members of the class, misbehaving in various ways. Sam thought the stranger was the cleverest artist he had ever seen.

'Do you draw pictures to make people laugh?' said Sam.

'Yes, and to inform them as well,' said the man. 'When you laugh, you learn without noticing.'

He glanced at his pocket watch. 'Actually, I've about done for the day and I must be going.' He bent down, picked up his pencil case and made towards the door. Then he stopped, smiled slightly, performed a mock bow in the boy's direction and said, 'By the way, Cruikshank's the name, George Cruikshank.' Another moment and he was gone.

After break, Sam learnt from Mr Macgregor that George Cruikshank was a famous artist who had illustrated many of Charles Dickens' novels. And like Dickens himself he did much valuable work for the Ragged School Union.

After a time in his new lodging Sam's promise to Dancing Poll, that he would visit her at Field Lane, started to bother him. The journey to Kensington had taken some time, even by horse and cart and he didn't see how he could find his way there on foot. On the other hand he did not want to let her down, so he decided to tell Tom.

'We'll go on Sunday,' said Tom. 'I know it's a long way but if we start off early we should be there before midday and then we've got the whole afternoon.'

So on Sunday, after breakfast, they set off on the walk to Holborn. By the time they'd had a long rest on a park bench and then been distracted by impromptu wrestling matches and then skimmed stones on a pond, the journey took about three hours. They arrived feeling they hadn't eaten for a week and of course, they had no money. Tom, who was always hungry, started complaining about being 'half starved', so Poll, who realized that the strange boy whom Sam hadn't introduced must be a friend, stepped in. She went to the kitchen and persuaded the cook to give them some bread. As she walked across the yard, Sam wondered how Poll kept herself so neat. After all, she dressed in cast-off clothes, just like him but they were neatly darned. Even her raven-coloured wavy hair was smartly combed and fastened down by a pin.

As they ate, the two boys could see that Poll was excited about something. 'I've got some news for you, Sam,' she said. 'When you were selected for the shoeblack brigade, I went to Mr White and asked if I could join too but he said they don't take girls. So I said I wanted to earn some money as well and he said, "Why not become a stepper?" That means a step girl. Anyway, he made enquiries and they accepted me. After I've been trained I'll be part of a brigade, with a uniform and able to knock on people's doors to ask if they want their step cleaned.'

'Where are they training you, Poll?' said Tom, trying to be friendly to the new companion who had helped fill his stomach.

'I'm not sure, Ox, Oxford something,' said Poll, uncertainly.

'Oxford Street,' said Tom, 'I bet it's Oxford Street. Our house is near there.'

'Yes, I think you're right,' said Poll, 'but it might all take a few weeks yet.'

'Listen, I've got an idea,' said Tom suddenly. 'Holborn's a long way from Kensington, a lot too far for a comfortable walk. Why don't we arrange a regular meeting at our place. It's about half way between. You can both meet my mum and granddad.'

Sam had no idea that Tom had a mother, let alone one with a house, but he thought it a good idea and so did Poll. And they arranged to meet there every Saturday afternoon. Tom gave Poll the address and some directions before the boys set off for their lodgings, where they finally arrived late in the evening.

In those days Oxford Street was a great coaching road, an extension of the Uxbridge Road, which led out into rural Middlesex, through the pretty villages of Shepherd's Bush, Acton, Ealing and Southall. All day long waggons and coaches clattered their way to and fro, bringing in produce from the farms and market gardens.

When Sam arrived on the first Saturday, after carefully following Tom's directions, he found himself on a small square within a stone's throw of London's wealthiest street. The area appeared deserted, apart from a single well-dressed couple hurrying through to a waiting carriage.

Then he noticed a group of ragged children standing silently outside a wooden hovel. One of them, a bare-foot boy of about eight, in an oversized peaked cap, stood with an arm about an emaciated young sister. The miserable patch of land in front of the houses was strewn with rubbish and covered in weeds.

There was a tiny tumbledown cottage on one corner of the square that matched his friend's description. The door was open so Sam walked in to find Poll and Tom already arrived. The inside was plain, with little furniture but it was spick and span, thanks to Tom's mother.

When her husband died she was left to raise Tom, two younger brothers and a sister on her own. So to make ends meet she moved into the cottage with her widowed father, a wounded veteran of Waterloo. The old man, an amputee, tried to make a living selling ribbons on street corners. Trade was poor at the best of times, so Tom was trying to earn money through shoe blacking. He wanted to give the younger children a good start in life.

Tom's mother, a strongly built woman with a snub nose and curly hair like her son, greeted Sam with a hug that took his breath away. 'Sit down, Sam, and make yourself at home. I'll fetch you some tea.'

It was that Saturday evening that the friendship between the three children began to deepen. Tom's mother made piles of toast over the open coal fire. Then they sat in the light of a flickering oil lamp, clutching mugs of steaming tea, taking it in turns to tell stories.

Tom's grandfather, a cheerful old man, kept the children spellbound, when he told of his adventures in the army. He had been with Wellington the whole time, first in Spain and then at Waterloo. That night and many another they stayed up till gone midnight listening to exciting stories of French cavalry charges foundering against British squares. Then they flopped exhausted on to their mattresses and slept deeply till morning.

It was after one such story-telling session that Sam told Tom and Poll about his prayers.

'I do it every day and at first I only prayed for a new mum and dad and I still do but now I also pray for you and for Poll.'

'Thank you, Sam, that's very nice of you, I'm really touched,' said Tom and Sam noticed the tears in his eyes. 'But what exactly do you pray about?'

'For you, I pray that you'll do really well as a shoeblack so you'll have the money to help the family. For Poll, I'm praying that her sister is found and that someone will come along to look after her,' replied Sam.

'What a good idea,' shouted Poll excitedly. 'We'll all pray for one another. I think we've all had such a tough time recently that we've forgotten that God is always on our side. And I know he is because Miss Stretton told me so.'

Gradually the weather got warmer and the days became longer. Then one morning in late April Rob Roy assembled his shoeblacks in the large hall of the ragged school.

'I have an announcement to make, lads,' he said.

'The last few weeks have been tough on ye and I worrked ye harrd but I did it for a purrpose.' Rob Roy paused for effect and Sam realized he was pleased with himself. He always slipped into broad Scottish when he was in a good mood.

'The time has come for the special job you all volunteered for before you came here. The fact is that tomorrow is the furrst of May, so your training is over and it's time for ye to make a living. Your new uniforms have come and I want ye to try them for size.' He indicated a large trunk by his side. 'Then furrst thing tomorrow, I'll take ye to ye place of worrk.'

It was some time before the urchins got the hang of their new clothes. Most of them had never dressed smartly before and had certainly never seen a whole row of buttons. It was also difficult to get both a uniform and a military style peaked cap of the right size but they managed in the end, with a lot of help from Mr Macgregor.

Then there was much posturing and laughter as they stood around jostling, admiring one another's uniforms and posing in front of the mirror. Finally, Rob Roy called them to order, adjusted a hat here and a jacket there and the squad was ready. It was time for the evening meal and early bed, ready for work in the morning.

Chapter 4
THE CRYSTAL PALACE

Sam noticed that Rob Roy had a slight smile on his face as he led them towards their workplace on a fine May day morning. The truth was that Mr Macgregor had planned a surprise for the boys. It was he who had thought of the idea of a shoeblack brigade in the first place and so they were his pride and joy. Sam had no way of knowing about the surprise, of course, but he suspected that something was about to happen.

The group of twenty-five boys in their smart new red uniforms proceeded at marching pace, in single file behind their leader. Sam had got used to thinking the area round the ragged school was affluent but he changed his mind as they neared the south side of Hyde Park. The streets were filled with people of rank and fashion and you could see liveried servants through the windows of stately homes. The only familiar sight was the occasional chimney sweep or street trader. Horses trotted past, their riders either army officers in bright uniforms or fine ladies travelling side saddle. They must be close now because Sam saw a group of children dancing round a Maypole in what could only be Hyde Park.

'Nearly there now,' Rob Roy called out over his shoulder. 'We turn in at the next gate, the one right by the barracks.'

As they wheeled sharp left through the gate into the park all the boys stopped dead. No one said anything and Tom just stared, his mouth gaping open. Then at last he spoke.

'What do you think it is?' he said to Sam.

'It could be something like a palace,' said Sam uncertainly, 'except that it looks as if it's made of glass. It must be a glass palace.'

Actually it was quite difficult to look directly at the building because of the reflections from thousands of glass panels. It reminded Sam of a glowing fairytale palace he had seen in a story book, back at Field Lane.

'Doesn't it look wonderful, lads? It's my little surprise for you and you're right Sam, it is made of glass. But we call it the Crystal Palace and in it there'll be the Great Exhibition of Works and Industry of all Nations, till October. We're expecting visitors from all over the world, as well as Britain, and your job is to clean their shoes.'

As they approached the building, Rob Roy continued with his commentary. 'We're headed for the south entrance, the one you can see in front of you. It will probably be the one most people use and today at noon, Her Majesty the Queen will come through it, to open the exhibition.'

They drew nearer to the Crystal Palace and began threading their way through groups of red-coated soldiers standing around the entrance. Some of them were already forming themselves into ranks in readiness for the royal visit. Instinctively Sam began to walk more upright and tried to imagine his brand-new shoeblack's outfit as a soldier's uniform.

'Do you think we look like soldiers?' he said to Tom.

Tom smiled. 'We might in a few years' time, Sam, but we've still got a lot of growing up to do.'

Mr Macgregor was speaking again. 'I want you all to look up at the flags on the roof. They're the flags of all the nations who have exhibits inside. Ours, the British one, is in the middle. As most of you already know, it's called the Union Flag.'

They had now arrived at the south entrance and Sam could see the booths where visitors bought their tickets. Rob Roy slipped inside to tell the organizers that the shoeblacks were reporting for duty. As they waited a coach drew up and a large lady had to be helped down by one of the coachmen. When she got to the entrance, the hem of her skirt was so wide that she couldn't get through the narrow opening. The boys watched with great interest as the two coachmen desperately tried to squeeze the angry woman through.

'Let go of my shoulder, you fool. Don't you dare tread on my toes. Mind my bonnet.'

Sam turned his head to see Mr Cruikshank in the background, sketchpad in hand, attempting to record the scene. 'These should go down well with my editor, Sam,' he smiled. 'It means my hungry family will have bread in their mouths for the next few weeks.'

'No time to lose, lads. We've got to take our places as quickly as possible. The royal party is on its way from Buckingham Palace.' Rob Roy beckoned the shoeblacks to follow him.

As they hurried through the strange structure of iron and glass, Sam had little time to study the exhibits. All he noticed were one or two statues and a large wrought iron gate in front of a spacious open area with a large tree at the back. Sam guessed that the tree had already been in the park and the Crystal Palace had been built around it.

'We've got to get to our places as quickly as we can,' said Mr Macgregor. An attendant indicated some metal stairs and they began to climb. The gallery at the top was already filling up fast, as the shoeblacks made their way through the crowd to the safety rail. From their new position they could see the other galleries also packed with spectators. Down below, just in front of the tree a platform had been placed.

43

'That's where the Queen and Prince Albert will be standing,' explained Rob Roy.

'Who are the others, in front of the platform?' said Sam.

'The old man with the white hair and red tunic, that's the Iron Duke, the Duke of Wellington. And next to him is the Archbishop of Canterbury.' Rob Roy continued right through the group, patiently explaining who each of them were. Sam was particularly interested in the exotic costumes of the Indian and Chinese guests, as well as those from the African continent.

By now the building was completely full and the shoeblacks could hardly hear themselves speak above the din. Quite suddenly the chatter was interrupted by a fanfare of trumpets from the south entrance.

'Dead on twelve o'clock. It's the royal party. No more talking now,' said their leader in a stage whisper.

The band started to play a slow stately tune and the spectators waited in anticipation of Queen Victoria's arrival. They did not have to wait long and the young queen with her husband, Prince Albert, soon appeared at the head of the procession. Just behind were two children, a boy in a kilt, about Sam's age, and a girl walking by his side.

'Those are the eldest royal children, Prince Albert Edward and his sister Victoria, the Princess Royal,' whispered Mr Macgregor. 'Do you like his kilt? It reminds me of when I was a lad,' chuckled Rob Roy.

The royal party, together with members of other royal families from all over Europe, took their place on the platform. When the Queen stepped forward to make her speech and declare the Great Exhibition open, Sam noticed how small and vulnerable she looked compared to the tall soldiers and dignitaries. It seemed strange that so slight a figure, who looked hardly more than a girl, should be the head of a great empire. With the speech over and the choir singing the Hallelujah Chorus, a very strange thing happened. A man dressed in colourful Chinese robes dashed out from the crowd and threw himself at the Queen's feet. For a few moments no one knew what to do and then one of the soldiers put his hand on his sword and took a step forward. The Duke of Wellington motioned him to stand back. The Queen just smiled down at the man while Prince Albert stood quite still, showing no response at all.

Then the Lord Chamberlain, one of the Queen's officials, looking red faced and rather harassed walked over and asked him to stand up. He then placed him between the Archbishop of Canterbury and the Duke of Wellington. The next day Sam found out the man was the owner of a Chinese junk, moored in the Thames. All he had wanted to do was meet the Queen.

After the opening ceremony the Queen and Prince Albert walked through the Crystal Palace waving to the crowds. When, at last, the royal visit was all over and the excitement had died down, it was time for Mr Macgregor to show the shoeblacks their work stations in the exhibition building.

'You are very keen on reading, Sam, so we'll put you here. You can be next to the statue of William Shakespeare, our greatest poet and playwright. He might inspire you in your school work,' Rob Roy smiled. Sam would be on his own during work hours, earning his own money. He could hardly wait.

Life seemed good to the waif who, just a few months ago, had been starving on the streets. The mornings spent cleaning shoes were hard work but he got used to it. In the afternoons he continued with his education at the ragged school. Tom's pitch in the great glass palace was near Sam's, and the older boy had developed his own style to help get more custom. Sam was fascinated by Tom's skill and so he watched him to improve his own technique.

Tom's customer was short and very fat and he was mopping his face with a handkerchief. Tom winked at Sam and then spoke.

'Good morning, sir, 'ave you 'ad a good time at the exhibition? Your shoes are looking very dirty, if you don't mind me saying so. It's a very dusty place, the Crystal Palace. Would you like me to polish 'em for you, sir?'

The gentleman looked slightly surprised to be addressed like that by a boy. Then his face broke into a friendly smile.

'Why, yes, boy, I do believe you're right. They certainly do need a good clean.'

He placed his foot on Tom's stool and Tom chatted to him as he worked.

Sam was very impressed by Tom's charm and he could tell the gentleman was too. When his shoes were sparkling like new, the man patted Tom on the head and put some coins in his box. Then, with a beaming smile, he pressed a tip into the palm of the boy's hand and wandered back through the throng.

'That's the way to do it. You talk to them a bit. Tell 'em how good they are. Make a few jokes and you double your takings,' Tom explained.

The weeks sped by and the summer came. Sometimes the temperature inside the great palace grew unbearable, even with some of the glass panels open. The conditions made work difficult and Sam was always glad of the afternoons in school, where he could sit down and rest. The customers were affected too, with many growing grumpy and irritable in the heat, and the boy found it difficult to earn the same money.

Despite the trials with the weather, Sam prospered and grew popular with nearly everybody. He also became stronger because of the regular meals at the hostel. It was a great day for him when he finally managed to cross the ladder in the gymnasium.

Even the boys who laughed when he fell, stood up and cheered. His reading improved daily and with some effort he began to understand the notices at the displays in the Exhibition.

By now Sam was an experienced shoeblack and he had cleaned the shoes of tall, sun-bronzed men from the United States, dusky Maharajahs from India, Chinese potentates and tall African chiefs. He was expert at talking to customers and was catching up Tom in the money he made.

Sometimes, when he had time to spare, Sam would wander round looking at the exhibits. Among his favourites was the Indian display with the largest diamond in the world, the Kohinoor. He also liked the United States department, with its statues of Red Indians in feathered head-dresses. There were new machines and strange inventions everywhere and he loved the brightly coloured fine tapestries of the Egyptian and Turkish rooms. There was history in the Medieval Court and without even making an effort he discovered he was learning more from the exhibition than he was from his school books.

The entrance fee to the Great Exhibition was five shillings, which meant most of the customers were from the middle and upper classes of Victorian England. Among themselves the shoeblacks called them the 'nobs'. Sam learnt how to get on with them but the best times were the shilling days when labouring people came. They were much more cheerful than their wealthy neighbours and they reminded Sam of his family and the poor people of Greenwich. Sam felt a warm glow when they came, the same glow remembered from his old home by the river. And the surprising thing was they wanted their shoes cleaned and were just as generous as the nobs. More generous if you took into account their income.

On the shilling days, the statue of Shakespeare was permanently surrounded by hordes of roughly spoken visitors, laden with baskets of food and drink. Some of the men had beer to drink and the women gin. Raucous laughter filled the air. Children ran everywhere, in and out of the crowd and around their parents' feet. Often the young women suckled babies.

It was on a shilling day that Sam first caught sight of a boy he had known in Greenwich. He was standing in the crowd round the statue and the young shoeblack caught him staring. As soon as he saw Sam looking he vanished into the crowd as quickly as he came. His face seemed familiar, yet Sam could not bring his name to mind. It wasn't until that evening, after much brooding, that he remembered him as an unpleasant, aggressive boy who had lived near the waterfront. He and his brothers had often been in trouble with the police for fighting and stealing. Sam was worried but he decided it was best to try and forget about the incident.

The next shilling day was a week later and Sam hadn't enjoyed himself so much for a long time. One of the visitors had won some money on a horse race and was determined to spend all of it at the exhibition. He bought Bath buns from the Refreshment Court and gave them out to everyone around the statue. Afterwards he amused them all with his jokes and funny stories.

Sam's face ached with laughter by the end of the morning and his stomach ached with buns. He was packing his equipment away when he felt a tap on his shoulder. He turned to find the unpleasant boy grinning behind him.

''Ullo, young un. Remember me then, Teddy Hudson?'

Sam felt flustered. 'Er, I don't know, well I think so.'

'Yeah, 'course you do. There ain't many from Greenwich who'd forget me an' me bruvvers. You ain't too proud to know your old mates, are you?'

'Well, no, not really,' said Sam, thinking just the opposite but he was afraid of the boy.

'Nice uniform you've got there, son.' He felt the cloth of Sam's jacket with a slight sneer on his face and Sam shrank away. 'I expect you make a bit too. Mind you, I bet you don't earn as much as me. I work for the Pineapple.'

Sam sucked in his breath sharply and began to choke. 'Steady on, old son. Don't get so worried. It ain't nothing to get upset about.'

Sam was upset, though, despite himself because he knew who the Pineapple was. It was his uncle, his father's brother, Pineapple Jack Clarke, one of the biggest villains south of the river. At one time he had earned an honest living as a costermonger, taking his donkey cart from market to market. He was successful too, a man of great charm who could sell anything to anybody. Uncle Jack made a lot of money selling pineapples, when most of the other traders were content with apples and oranges. But he was also cruel and dishonest with a vicious temper.

One night, after drinking heavily, he got into a knife fight with a fellow trader and the man had almost died of stab wounds but not before he scarred Jack's face.

The other costermongers said nothing to the police; they were a close community who dealt with their own problems. But they barred Jack from all the markets, so he couldn't work any more and turned to crime.

'The Pineapple's moved north now, crossed the Thames. Greenwich weren't big enough for him and he wanted to expand. 'E 'eard you was in 'ere, 'cos I told 'im an' 'e wants you to come and work for 'im, bein' as you're family, like.'

At last Sam found his voice and he heard it tremble slightly. 'But I don't want to work for Uncle Jack. My mum warned me about him and said he was a thief and scoundrel who would come to a bad end. Dad didn't like him either. I've got friends now and I've got a job. I don't want to be a thief. So go away and leave me alone.'

Teddy stepped back, his face red with anger. 'Right, if that's the way you want it. I was only trying to help, that's all. I thought you'd be glad to see some of your old mates from Greenwich. I tell you this for nothin', though, the Pineapple ain't gonna like it.' The boy turned and stormed off in a huff.

After that Sam became nervous and withdrawn and started having nightmares. One night he started shouting in his sleep and Tom asked him what was wrong. Sam was reluctant to say at first but in the end he told Tom everything. The older boy was horrified at the thought of losing his friend to a criminal, so he asked for volunteers among the shoeblacks to help protect Sam. By the time Tom had finished there was always at least one volunteer keeping watch while Sam was in the Crystal Palace. Little by little, with the help of his friends he calmed down and the incident began to fade from his mind. The young waif began to feel that life was worth living once more.

Chapter 5
PINEAPPLE JACK

Late one morning, soon after the Teddy Hudson affair, Sam was thinking of packing his equipment away when he noticed a uniformed soldier staring at him. The boy was nervous, especially after the recent incident, but he was also curious. So he decided to carry on as normal and see what happened, rather than call the other shoeblacks to his aid. In the event, his curiosity was quickly satisfied because within minutes the man was by his side.

'Do you think you could cope with a pair of army boots?' the other enquired.

'I think so, sir,' said Sam politely, 'that's one of the things we were trained to do.'

As the young shoeblack applied the polish he began to glance at his unusual customer to see if he posed a threat. Close up, he seemed younger than Sam had first assumed; probably in his early thirties, the boy thought. His features were even and he was clean shaven, apart from bushy brown sideburns. Sam thought him ruggedly good looking and he was certainly powerfully built. Sam guessed from the cut of the uniform and his confident bearing that he was an officer of some sort. He must have started to stare, because the soldier smiled at him.

'What's your name, boy?' he said, in gentle tones.

'Sam, sir,' said the boy, wondering if he was in trouble.

'And how old are you, Sam?'

'Ten, sir. Excuse me but aren't you hot in all those clothes?' The soldier was in full dress uniform of high necked red tunic with epaulettes, black knee-length boots, white breeches and a black shiny peaked cap or shako. By his side was a large sword in a sheath, which hung awkwardly by the side of the chair.

'On a warm day like this, certainly, and all these windows don't help. But I'm on duty, you see, the London regiments are taking it in turns to guard important people who come to the exhibition and at the moment the responsibility is ours. Once you're in the army you get used to not being comfortable most of the time,' the officer chuckled. He had an easy way with him that made Sam feel at ease.

The pair were joined by a sad-looking woman about the same age as the soldier. 'Ah, there you are my dear,' she said, 'I've been looking for you everywhere.'

'I got rather held up, I'm afraid. Sam here has been cleaning my shoes. He's ten years old, Charlotte, my love, the same age as William would have been.'

The unhappy look in the woman's eyes increased. 'My husband had a son who would have been your age but he died of cholera, along with two brothers and a sister. Their mother, my husband's first wife, died shortly afterwards. It's been an absolutely terrible period for him and even now he's melancholy much of the time. Whether he'll ever get over it, I'm sure I don't know.'

'It'll take time, my love, but I'm sure I will and meeting you has made up for a lot of it already. But Sam really does look a lot like William,' replied the officer. His wife sighed softly but said nothing.

'Well, I suppose we must be off, can't keep you talking when you've a living to earn,' he said to Sam as he put a generous sum into the box. 'Lieutenant and Mrs Richard Hopwood of Blackwall, at your service,' beamed the soldier. 'Goodbye Sam, you did the boots well.'

'Goodbye sir, goodbye ma'am,' said Sam, waving his hand as the couple mingled with the crowds and then disappeared from view.

In a few weeks Pineapple Jack and all he stood for were nearly forgotten and Sam busied himself with his job. He was now an expert at all aspects of shoe polishing, and customers who returned to the exhibition often asked for him by name. Then one day he recognized two of the older urchins from the dry arch. He was about to greet them when he noticed Teddy Hudson with a bigger boy walking right behind. Sam racked his brains and finally remembered— it was Teddy's older brother Alfie.

Something about the furtive way the group moved told Sam they were up to mischief and probably working together as criminals. As he watched, he saw Teddy jostle a portly gentleman while Alfie attempted to pick his pocket. They failed because the victim was wary and guarded his pockets with his hands. Several attempts were made on other visitors and then, at last, a purse was taken from a lady's bag. She was completely unaware of what happened and poor Sam simply didn't know what to do for the best.

He was frightened, particularly of Teddy and Alfie, because of their connection with Pineapple Jack. But, on the other hand, he didn't want them to get away with it. Really he ought to find a policeman to tell but he was confused. Because of his time on the streets he was afraid of the police. There was only one person he could turn to and that was Tom, so Sam ran across and said what he'd seen. He pointed out the culprits and Tom, normally the most cheerful of boys, exploded with anger. Taking no thought for his personal safety he rushed at Alfie, waving his arms and shouting. Then he seized the boy tightly by the collar and held on, like a bull terrier gripping his prey. There was pandemonium as the other pickpockets tried to free their companion but Tom was determined not to let go. Sam joined in and grabbed Alfie's legs. A bewildered crowd gathered and then an attendant sent for the police. A burly officer arrived and placed one hand on Tom and the other on Alfie and lifted them both in the air. The pickpockets vanished silently into the crowd.

'Well, now, and what are you two boys fighting about?' said the policeman, red-faced with exertion.

'They weren't fighting. Tom here arrested a pickpocket,' shouted Sam frantically.

The policeman slowly turned his head and looked at Sam. 'And who, exactly, are you son? How am I to tell if you're speaking the truth? After all, I've never clapped eyes on you before.'

'Well, Tom and me are both shoeblacks; we work here. It's just that our uniforms got dirty with all that rolling on the floor. If you don't believe me ask Mr Macgregor over at the Ragged School,' said Sam indignantly.

'Ah, so you're one of the Shaftesbury boys,' said the policeman, now perspiring freely. He released his hold on Tom while keeping a firm grip on Alfie. 'I know John Macgregor and he always informs the police whenever he starts something new. We all trust him because he trains boys to work and not run the streets. And we know he's careful only to choose the best for shoeblacks. I'd rather believe you than him.' He nodded at Alfie and then carefully searched him, finding not only the purse but several items of jewellery as well. 'Come on you young scoundrel, you're under arrest.'

The policeman held up the articles for the onlookers to see and shouted, 'Does anyone own these?' One or two people murmured among themselves but nobody came through the crowd to claim them.

'We could have a problem here, son,' said the officer to Sam, 'no one admits to ownership and you are the only witness. Still, you can come along to the police station and make a statement, then we'll see what the magistrate says in court.'

As Sam and Tom followed the policeman, and his struggling prisoner, out of the building, Sam noticed Teddy at the back of the throng, staring at him, his face contorted with rage. As they left, he shook his fist and shouted something threatening that the young shoeblack couldn't quite hear. Sam was frightened and even when he returned for afternoon school he was still trembling.

Tom, now the hero of the lodging house, did his best to comfort him and promised to stay close for the next few days. But Tom was not confident he could cope on his own, so he told John Macgregor who then informed the police. An officer was assigned to keep an eye on Sam quietly as he went about his work.

'And I think it might be an idea if we prayed for Sam's safety. The last thing we want is for him to get mixed up with some of the criminal gangs you get in this area,' said Rob Roy. 'And don't think I haven't noticed that you and young Sam have started praying together, without any prompting from me, and I must say I'm very pleased.' Mr McGregor smiled and squeezed Tom's shoulder to encourage him.

The following day, when Sam and Tom had finished for the morning, they left the exhibition hall only with great difficulty, because of the large crowd that had gathered for an important guest. The visitor was Sir Joseph Paxton, a famous gardener who had designed the Crystal Palace as a giant greenhouse. They headed south towards the Prince of Wales Gate, the one they used on their first day. The watching policeman saw them go but he had no orders to follow Sam out of the building.

The problem was that the scurrying crowd was really in two sections, one that wanted the south and another that pushed north. The two boys somehow got in different streams and became separated. A despairing Sam caught a glimpse of Tom's shock of brown hair, disappearing into the throng before losing sight of him completely.

Sam was caught up in a surging current of humanity and was powerless to get out of it. He crossed Rotten Row, where riders would normally have been out with their horses. The Serpentine Lake was to his right and he soon found himself walking across the narrow footbridge. Just below were happy families splashing about in rowing boats but Sam had no time to stand and stare. He wanted to cry but he hunched his shoulders and made for the north side of the park.

The crowd began to spread out and thin, as people headed for different exit gates and Sam turned round with the intention of waiting for the bridge to clear. Then he could head back south and rejoin Tom. He glanced anxiously at the blank faces of those leaving the exhibition, hoping either to recognize a friend or see an enemy and then take avoiding action.

His stomach churned with fear but everything seemed safe and no one threatening appeared, so he slowly retraced his steps. He reached a large oak near to the bridge, stopped and took cover behind its trunk. A flock of sheep stopped their chewing and cantered off into the distance. Sam froze and hoped they hadn't revealed his presence. Then he carefully peered out and was able to view those crossing the Serpentine. And there was Teddy, not actually heading towards the oak but at least walking in a northerly direction.

Sam began to sweat but had no way of knowing whether the young pickpocket was following him or whether he was heading home, but something had to be done quickly. There were still large numbers of people making for the gates and Sam decided to use them as cover while making for the Uxbridge Road, the northern boundary of Hyde Park.

Once he reached there he could turn left, past Kensington Gardens, keeping out of sight among the pedestrians on the footways. Then he could move south again by skirting Kensington Palace and be back at the lodging house before anyone realized he was missing.

Sam managed to work his way in front of a large and noisy working-class family consisting of a mother, father, aunts, uncles and several children. He could see Teddy in the distance but as far as he could tell, the pickpocket hadn't spotted him. Sam left the park by the Albion Gate, then turned to see if he was being followed.

There was the young rogue with his two companions of the previous day. They still appeared not to have seen him but Sam panicked and ran across the Uxbridge Road, narrowly avoiding being run down by a hansom cab. The driver cracked his whip and shouted at Sam who cursed himself for his stupidity. Now he had drawn attention to his flight. Really frightened, the boy scampered into a side street and ran for his life. After several minutes, when he felt safe, he slowed, glanced round to make sure he wasn't followed and darted down an alleyway.

He thought he heard footsteps behind so he broke into a run once more. Half way along was another alley, running at right angles to his. He turned into it and the footsteps became more definite. Then, to his horror he found himself in a dead end. There was a brick wall about ten feet high in front of him and he could see no way of escape. Sam turned to see who was following but no one was visible. He could make out moving shadows, from figures just out of sight, at the entrance to the alley. Then a horse and cart came into view and blocked the opening so that nobody could pass.

Sam edged a little closer, hoping to make a quick dash for freedom. From his new position, within a few feet of the cart, he saw that the horse was really a donkey. And not any old donkey, there was something familiar about it, something he half remembered from long ago. It was the ears that gave it away. One was short and withered at the end, the result of an accident when the animal was just a foal. Then there was the look on the face, a kind of sulky, grumpy look, as if it were out of sorts with the world. Yes, there was no doubt about it, it was Carrots, his uncle's donkey.

Sam's heart sank at first but the boy quickly recovered and even felt elated. With Carrots, there were no half measures, he either loved you or hated you and usually it was the latter. But Sam was an exception, the animal loved him. The boy had always made a fuss of Carrots, whenever he went to his uncle's house, in the old days, before Jack turned to crime. Even the cart looks familiar, thought Sam, it must be the old coster cart. The driver, known to Sam from the dry arch days, was staring at him, waiting for him to make a move. From the shadows beyond the opening Sam knew that two others lay in wait. The boy was quite calm now. He took a deep breath, sprinted for the cart, ducked his head, was underneath and out the other side before anybody else could move.

Dodging swiftly from side to side he made for the street. With the good food from the lodging house and Tom's coaching, Sam's fitness had improved and he felt elated as he outdistanced his pursuers. The floor of the ancient alleyway was made of gravel, with broken rocks right below the surface. And that was Sam's undoing because, as he reached the street, a jutting rock tripped him and his ankle turned. The boy sprawled face down and the world went black. He lay stunned and breathless, and as he came to, he was aware of powerful hands hauling him to his feet. With one on each arm and Teddy with a hand clamped across his mouth, he was frogmarched back to the cart.

By now the young shoeblack had begun to recover and was thinking very clearly. Teddy became over confident and allowed the tip of his thumb to stray into Sam's mouth. The plucky youngster seized his opportunity and bit as hard as he could. Teddy screamed and let go, then rolled on the ground, yelling and moaning.

'The young varmint, he bit my thumb. I think he's broke it,' yelled Teddy.

'You wait till the Pineapple hears about this,' sneered the youth on the cart. 'You can't even hold a ten year old. Jack'll rip yer thumbs off for being so stupid.'

Teddy said nothing at all but started whimpering softly to himself and Sam noticed his cheeks were stained with tears. Then suddenly he made a lunge for the driving seat, grabbed the whip and launched himself at Sam. The impact knocked the boy to the ground and the two wrestled beneath Carrot's feet. At this point, Carrots noticed the whip in Teddy's hand and Carrots was a donkey who bore a grudge. So as they staggered to their feet, still grappling, he unleashed an almighty kick at the pickpocket's shin. Once more Teddy doubled up, screaming in agony, while Sam made good his escape. But he wasn't quite quick enough and the other two, tired of Teddy's incompetence cornered him in the alleyway.

One of them had a length of string and they used it to bind Sam's arms to his sides. Then they slipped a piece of rough sacking over his head and bundled him on to the cart. He felt the hard wooden boards against his face, then old rags were piled on top of him and he was obscured from the world, weeping quietly in frustration.

'Sorry Sam,' he heard one of them say, 'but orders is orders. And you, Teddy,' he said in an aggressive tone, 'stop snivelling about your leg.' Abruptly the whining stopped and the cart began to move. A red-eyed Teddy, his body racked by hiccupping sobs, sat next to the driver. The other was in the back with Sam, making sure he didn't wriggle free and drop down to the ground. Sam gritted his teeth and decided crying was no use. He determined not to yell for help, as passers-by were unlikely to want to get involved with three ruffians on a cart. And in any case, the three were the kind who yelled and shouted in public as a matter of habit, so it might be assumed that they were merely behaving as expected.

Instead he listened to try and discover the way they were going. The noise of traffic on the Uxbridge Road gradually receded and then the bumping of the cart told him that they were moving over cobbles. They turned right and then left, and at one point he heard a church clock striking. But the journey did not take long, perhaps a quarter of an hour at most, even at Carrot's normal walking pace. This was snail's pace by the standards of most donkeys, as he greatly resented having to pull a cart at all.

When they finally stopped, Sam was seized by his captors, carried bodily into a nearby house and up some stairs at high speed. A door was opened, he was stood on his feet, the sacking removed, the string cut and then the door was slammed shut.

Sam was all alone and at first he felt dizzy. Then he recovered his balance and began to rub his wrists where the bonds had dug in. He had pins and needles quite badly and it took some time for feeling to return to his hands. He examined his surroundings and found he was in a small room, stacked high with broken boxes and general junk. There had been a ceiling at one time but now you looked up and saw the underside of the roof. Some of the tiles were missing and Sam could see the sky in places but he dismissed the roof as an escape route. It was too high and there were no toe holds in the wall.

The room's solitary window was boarded up but he could see out, a little, to a fenced yard below. It's probably at the back of the house, thought Sam, and he saw Carrots being unhitched from the cart, which was then pushed against the fence. He could also hear movement and muffled speech from the room below, so he knew the house was occupied by people he had never seen.

Fairly close he could see a church steeple and guessed it was where he heard the clock. So we're not far from Hyde Park and the West End, the boy thought. Jack probably picked this place for the number of wealthy people living close by. But not so close that the house could easily be traced, mused Sam.

There seemed to be no way of escape and Sam felt so low he slumped in the corner and began to question his belief in God. All his hopes of a better life were gone; he was just a captive in a den of thieves. 'What's the point in believing in a God who doesn't help you when you need him?' said Sam to himself.

He must have remained locked away for several hours, before he heard the street door open and a familiar voice call out. There was a brief muffled discussion, then footsteps on the stairs. The door crashed open and there, framed in the doorway, stood his uncle, Pineapple Jack Clarke.

Chapter 6

THE HOUSE THAT JACK BUILT

'Sam, it's been a long time, 'ow are yer, boy? My, how you've growed. You know I wouldn't 'ave recognized yer if I'd a passed yer by in the street. Last time I seen yer, yer was knee 'igh to a grasshopper. Must a been, what, two or three year ago?'

Pineapple Jack shook his nephew's hand then clamped his other hand on Sam's shoulder. He was trying to appear friendly. Sam thought it safer to say nothing, in case he annoyed Jack by appearing critical.

'Anyway, why have they stuck you up 'ere, out of the way? Come down into my parlour an' we'll 'ave a little chat about old times.' Jack led Sam down the stairs into a room of such squalor that at first the boy found it difficult to find space to sit. Piles of rags and stacks of old newspapers were everywhere. In places, plaster had fallen from the walls and formed heaps by the skirting boards. Sam glanced up and saw parts of an upstairs room through holes in the ceiling. Thick cobwebs that drooped from the corners also managed to block most of the light from the window. Layers of grime covered every surface. A broken-down table, with a missing leg and supported one side by a pile of bricks, had the remains of a half-eaten meal still on it. Flies buzzed around an old chop bone and a mouse nibbled the stale crumbs that had fallen to the floor. The smell of damp rags, rotten food and unwashed bodies was difficult to stomach and Sam, who was now used to clean living conditions, actually felt sick.

Sam finally settled on an upturned orange box while Jack chose a bundle of newspapers, then leaned back against a heap of rags and sighed with contentment. He attempted a smile but the best he could manage was a twisted leer. As he did so, his long coat opened to reveal the hilt of a long, razor-sharp dagger. The cuffs of the coat had long since frayed, leaving ragged ends. He sniffed, wiped a cuff across his nose and started to speak.

'Well, nevvy, what do yer think of the old gaff, then? It could do with a lick o' paint 'ere an' there, granted, but basically it ain't at all bad.'

Sam grunted in a non-committal kind of way and took stock of his uncle. The years have not dealt with him kindly, thought Sam, he's aged a lot since I last saw him. Jack had several days' stubble on his chin and his ginger hair seemed to have fallen out in tufts, leaving bald patches on his scalp. A livid scar, from the knife fight, ran from the bottom of his left cheek to the underside of his eye, which had half closed, causing a permanent grimace. His teeth, intact and fairly even not that long ago, were reduced to brown snags by the ravages of tobacco smoke and poor hygiene.

The peaked costermonger's cap, once his pride and joy, had been taken off and balanced on his knee. It looked threadbare, having lost most of its sequins over the years.

The street door opened and a small, nervous-looking woman, in a flowered dress and a bonnet, entered the room. She carried a basket of groceries over her arm and as she looked up, Sam saw the dark bruise on her face.

The woman smiled in recognition. 'Why, as I live and breathe, it's young Sam,' she said, kissing him on the cheek. From close up the boy noted the food and drink stains, down the front of what had once been a pretty dress. It hadn't seen a darning needle for a long time and his aunt had been such a neat woman.

'Aunty Carrie, nice to see you,' said Sam, feeling relieved at a friendly face in strange surroundings. He had always got on well with Carrie, that is, when she was allowed to be herself by her bullying husband.

'Come on now, woman, you ain't got no time to stand around talking all day, get in that kitchen an' let's 'ave some grub,' snarled Jack. She said nothing but cast her eyes down and then sidled nervously away, leaving the man and boy together in the parlour. Sam's feeling of relief subsided. Aunty Carrie was much too afraid of Jack to be any help.

'Well I can't say I'm pleased with you Sam, 'cos I ain't. You've been a big disappointment to me, yer own flesh and blood. You would have stood witness against one of me best boys. I'll have to learn you a few lessons, I can see,' said Jack in a voice that sounded sorrowful rather than angry. Sam felt relieved, at least he hadn't yet felt the full force of his uncle's rage.

Suddenly Jack brightened. 'I tell you what I'll do. I'll show you round the place, so's you can see what it's like.' He stood up and indicated a door with his grimy finger. 'We'll go this way first and I'll introduce you to Mickey.' He ushered Sam into the next room, where a man sat at a table, looking thoughtful, pen in hand. 'This is Mickey my screever; 'is job is to write begging letters to the gentry, saying as how hard up he is. At the moment, he's writing to every member of the 'ouse of Lords, claiming to be a naval captain wounded in battle, who don't 'ave enough to support 'is wife an' kids. When the money comes rollin' in, I gets most of it but I gives 'im some for booze. Worth 'is weight in gold, is Mickey. 'Ad a good education too, went to Cambridge for a time till they caught him with his 'and in someone's wallet. Mickey's a drunk you see. He'll do anything for a pint o' beer.' The man stared blankly up at Sam and nodded briefly, then continued writing.

Sam looked at Mickey and noticed for the first time the effect that drink can have on someone's looks. The screever was probably in his thirties or early forties but the lank unkempt hair, the blotchy face and the filthy clothes aged him to sixty years or more.

As the boy watched, Mickey slumped forward on to the table, eyes closed and began to snore heavily. Unbalanced by the impact of Mickey's head, the tankard toppled on to its side, emptying beer all over the table top. From there it dripped on the floor and splattered on to some begging letters. The Pineapple said nothing but gave a sneer, then kicked the sleeping man's chair.

They were soon in the back yard and Sam was allowed to pet Carrots, and feed him his favourite vegetable. Observing Jack with his donkey made the boy realize that Carrots was the only creature in the world, human or otherwise, his uncle had ever loved. While aggression and brutality were his usual way there was only gentleness as he rubbed the animal's back with a piece of old sacking and fondled his ears.

'It's an old farmhouse, this place, of course it was all farms round 'ere at one time but now it's just wasteland. In a few years there'll be houses everywhere, 'cos it's so close to the West End an' all that money. Come up on the roof with me and I'll show you somethin',' said Jack, indicating a ladder leaning against a wall.

The roof was as poorly maintained as the rest of the house, with loose tiles making Sam think he was going to fall, but he was agile enough to keep his balance. The Pineapple was pointing into the distance.

'Over there boy, what can yer see?' Sam looked, and there in the distance, behind the trees of Hyde Park, he could see the Crystal Palace, as clear as day, its glass panels glinting in the evening sunshine. Horseback riders and pedestrians in the park could easily be seen, going about their business.

Suddenly the Pineapple looked across at Sam and began to ooze sentimentality. He had evidently decided the soft approach was the best way to gain the boy's confidence. The iron fist could come later if necessary.

'You're your father's son, me own flesh and blood an' I wants to 'elp yer. If yer work 'ard yer could come into all this when I'm dead and gorn. You could inherit, like.'

Sam caught the smell of Jack's unwashed body and thought, with horror, of the squalid farmhouse but his uncle continued speaking. 'Why, if yer puts yer shoulder to the wheel you could grow up to be like me.' The Pineapple grew pensive and deftly removed a morsel of food from his teeth with the point of his dagger. Sam looked down into the rafters where a tile had been displaced. A rat scuttled across the floor and into the skirting board.

The other rooms were similar to the parlour, showing the same degree of filth and misery. The sleeping quarters were all upstairs, except that there were no beds or even mattresses. It seemed you just lay down and slept anywhere you liked, whenever you felt tired. The only exceptions were one room for Jack and Carrie, and another for Mickey and his wife Sal.

'I've gotta go an' see Aunty Carrie, now,' announced Jack, when the tour of the house was complete. He used the word aunty as if he were a normal uncle talking to his nephew about family affairs. 'Only she's gotta go to the police station and get Alfie freed, now that there ain't no witnesses. I'd go myself only I'm too well known. Not that I'm a coward or nothin'.'

Late in the evening the house had filled with boys and youths of all descriptions, gathered in Jack's parlour to share out their spoils. The Pineapple had placed a large chest on the floor in front of him and items of jewellery, snuff boxes, purses and wallets were thrown in by the thieves. Clothing and handkerchiefs were put in a separate pile. Jack examined everything closely and then rewarded the donor with money. Sam could see the amounts given were far less than the goods were worth but none dared complain.

The front door opened and Carrie walked in with Alfie. Everyone cheered wildly and there was uproar for a time as Alfie was mobbed by friends. Even Jack found it difficult to calm things down and he had to wait till the excitement died away. The only people not involved were Mickey the screever and Sal, who were both so drunk they slept through the whole affair.

'How did it go, Alfie, with you an' the Peelers? You didn't tell 'em nothin, did yer?' said Jack. 'Only I wouldn't like it if you peached on us.'

'No, no, I never said nothin',' said Alfie nervously. 'You know me, Jack, I wouldn't.' The Pineapple said nothing but fixed him with a hard stare for several seconds, till the youth looked away. 'I never answered their questions and the only other time they spoke was when Carrie came. They said as 'ow you was a coward, sendin' yer wife along to do yer dirty work and that 'anging was too good for yer. One of 'em said he'd like to string you up 'is self.'

Pineapple Jack audibly gulped and placed his fingertips against his Adam's apple. 'Oh, that's very nice that is, typical of the esclop. I spends me life, workin' me fingers to the bone, taking boys off o' the streets and givin' 'em work to do and that's all the thanks I get.' His voice caught for a moment and he paused to fight back tears of self-pity. 'It's my fault really, I suppose. If I've got a weakness in my character it's being too soft, too kind 'earted. I'm a fool to myself sometimes, the way I always try to please. But there you are, someone's gotta take responsibility for the nation's yoof.'

He would have carried on but suddenly he caught sight of Teddy. 'I've gotta bone to pick wiv you, young man. What do yer mean by takin' a whip to my donkey? 'E got you back though, didn't 'e?' laughed Jack, looking at a purple lump the size of a hen's egg on the boy's shin.

'I never meant to whip Carrots, Pineapple,' said the frightened boy. 'I was goin' to hit Sam.' But it was no use, the Pineapple removed his heavy leather belt and took out the full weight of his fury on the boy. The onlookers were all afraid to intervene but when it was all finished, Alfie helped his whimpering brother upstairs.

In his room that night, Sam searched in his jacket pocket and found what he was looking for. It was his shoe scraper, a tool with a flat blade, used to remove mud from shoes. He'd dropped the rest of his shoe-cleaning kit in his flight across the Uxbridge Road but was glad he kept his scraper. After an hour or so he managed to prise up one end of a board that had been nailed across the window. There was no glass and the boy was small enough to wriggle through, once a board was taken out. Now his wrist was aching, so he hid the scraper and settled down to sleep. Escape would have to wait till tomorrow.

In the morning they breakfasted on stale cakes that one of the boys had stolen the day before. Sam overheard Pineapple telling Alfie and Teddy to 'try a little footpadding'. So when Teddy came in for breakfast, Sam asked him what Jack had meant.

'Footpadding, well, yer pleases yerself 'ow yer does it but Alfie and me gets a brick from the pile in the yard. Then we stands around near an alleyway and waits till a likely looking cove comes along and there ain't no one else about. Then we says, "wanna buy this brick, mister" and so 'e has to empty 'is pockets to buy the brick. And then if we're in the mood we lets 'im go but sometimes we 'its 'im with the brick anyway.' Sam noted the vicious look on Teddy's white, tear-stained face and realized that somebody was in for trouble that day.

'Sam, Jack says you've got to put these clothes on, only yer uniform's too bright and we've got work to do on the streets.' It was Aunty Carrie, and after he had changed, and she had made sure Jack was not about, she grabbed Sam's arm and started speaking in a low voice. 'I'm sorry boy, your mother would 'ate me if she was 'ere now but it's Jack you see. He'd half kill me if I didn't do as I was told; you've seen that knife he carries and he keeps guns as well. He's got them in a cupboard upstairs. Don't trust 'im, Sam, I know he acts all nice an' charmin' but 'e's vicious.' She looked round furtively. 'This is not the only place he's got; he keeps most of 'is loot in a hideaway. It's our old 'ouse over in Greenwich.' She looked up to see her husband approaching and moved away from Sam.

'Take young Ernie along with yer. He'll show Sam what to do,' said Jack with a menacing stare at Carrie. Ernie was a fresh-faced cheerful boy who looked about eight years old. He nodded at Sam, who smiled back weakly.

Carrie, Sam, Ernie and a hulking lout, acting as minder, made their way along Oxford Street to the destination that Jack had planned for them. Sam knew Oxford Street from his visits to Tom's house but today he did not enjoy the smart shops with their fashionable shoppers.

Just a few streets away was the row of villas that was to be the scene of the crime. From the alley behind, Carrie was able to make her choice of house. Then the lout lifted Sam and Ernie over the wall before positioning himself at the end of the row.

'You keep yer orbs peeled at the back door in case anybody comes out and I'll do the rest. Shout if there's trouble and we all run like mad,' said Ernie with a mischievous grin on his face. He was clearly enjoying his life of crime. Sam peered in through the back door but all he could see was an empty kitchen. In the meantime Ernie was removing some expensive-looking washing from the clothes line. They were the kind of garments that the poor of London could only dream about and would fetch a good price in the second-hand markets.

Ernie threw the clothes over his shoulder and then passed them to Carrie across the wall. Carrie put them in her basket and then whistled the lookout. He lifted the two boys back into the alley and the group walked back into the street. The lookout stayed on watch, some little distance behind the others.

During the course of the day they performed the same trick several times until the basket was full. At one time a policeman stopped to pass the time of day with Carrie. He even sympathized about the weight of the washing she had to carry. But he was not suspicious because it was common enough to see a woman with two young children and a basket of laundry. Jack knew how to exploit people's weaknesses when he planned criminal activities.

Later, locked in his room, Sam kept thinking of Tom and Dancing Poll, something he did often. He saw them in his mind's eye, in school or at the house with Tom's mother. Are they wondering where I am or have they forgotten me? he thought, and it cast a gloom over him. Then he shook himself into action. This wasn't the time to sit around and mope.

He had to work quickly with his shoe scraper, and about midnight by the church clock he removed the plank from the window. He stuck his head out and looked at the outhouse just below. A short drop and he would be on the roof. Then away to the wasteland, Hyde Park and the lodging house.

He wriggled through the opening and lowered himself on to the tiles. His foot slipped as he jumped to the ground and a tile clattered on to the yard. He stood still for several minutes but there was no one about, except Mickey who was fast asleep on the outhouse floor.

Sam padded silently across the yard until he reached Carrot's stable and thought he saw a shadow. He looked up startled and his eyes widened at the figure before him. There stood Pineapple Jack, hands on hips, watching him. The boy felt sick to the stomach, all his dreams of escape had come to nothing. He tried his best to hold back the bitter salt tears but he just wasn't strong enough and within seconds the dam burst. Sam began to cry in great gasping sobs that simply refused to die away, until the long night was over and the sun was high in the sky.

Chapter 7
POLL SEES IT THROUGH

After his escape attempt Sam was confined to the farmhouse for several weeks. He made a point of saying nothing about the affair, unless pressed. It was during his period of captivity that he discovered a faith in God as a loving father and protector. Somehow he knew that whatever happened in the days and weeks to come, God would always be with him. It was just like in the Twenty-third Psalm that he'd heard Rob Roy recite so many times in ragged school: 'thy rod and thy staff they comfort me'. Every night, as he made ready to sleep in his lonely room, he'd say his prayers. In the end Jack decided it was safe to let him out but only under certain conditions. At the evening share-out of spoils, Pineapple announced that Sam would be rejoining Carrie and her linen thefts but that he would be closely guarded until he could be trusted.

This seemed to annoy Teddy who thought Sam should have been punished more. But the truth was that Jack did not want to punish Sam too severely because he had heard the police were searching for the boy. He knew the search might continue for some time, because it was urged on by John Macgregor. If Sam was found he hoped to get off lightly and claim he was only giving a home to his nephew.

'Linen stealing is women's work, why aren't yer learning him to footpad like me an' Alfie?' said the young rascal indignantly. It was a foolish thing to say, because he caught Jack on a raw nerve.

'It's nothin' to do with women's work, he's just startin' off small, that's all. There ain't nothing to be ashamed of in that. I started small, down at the street market in Greenwich. I used to offer to look after the donkeys when the costers wanted to go for a drink. And I charged 'em for it. The only thing was, the donkeys wasn't in no danger, apart from me. If they refused to pay up, I'd whack the animal on the rump and off he'd run.' Jack must have been highly amused by his wit because he gave a phlegmy laugh, which rapidly turned to a hacking cough. He ended up choking and spluttering for several minutes, unable to speak.

The assembled gang sat dumbstruck, not knowing whether to laugh at the joke, or try to appear concerned at his plight. At any rate it saved Teddy from another beating, because Pineapple had forgotten the remark by the time he recovered. Sam went to his room that night with a feeling of great sadness; he was being sucked back into the underworld again and by the following day he would be helping to commit a crime.

Oxford Street had changed since his last visit. The shops were preparing for Christmas, festive crowds thronged the pavements and there was a seasonal chill in the air. Sam remembered that his father had died about a year ago. He thought of the emptiness of life on the streets and all that had happened since his capture. There seemed no obvious way of escape for the moment.

His head buzzed with ideas that led nowhere, so he just looked around for ways of making things awkward for his companions. Then, given half a chance he would escape. He also decided to make the most of his chance to see Oxford Street at Christmas. So he took every opportunity to slow down, dawdle and examine the displays in the shop windows.

There was a bright butcher's shop with plump geese, turkeys and pheasants hanging in the window. On the slab below were joints of Christmas beef and pork. Huge strings of sausages had been cleverly threaded in and out between them. The window's edges were expertly decked with holly and mistletoe to lend an air of seasonal jollity.

Even the neighbouring greengrocer's, humble by Oxford Street standards, was stocked with pyramids of tangerines and oranges. On the pavement outside were baskets of English cobnuts and figs from the Mediterranean.

In places, the throng of shoppers was so great that Sam found it difficult to walk on the pavement, so he edged out into the road. He considered a dash for freedom; the lookout had a reputation for idleness but he was out of luck. The youth grabbed his arm, steered him back to the line of shop fronts and then held on to him for some time.

As the group pressed on through the gloom, Sam stopped at a large baker's shop, where wooden trays were filled with mince pies, Christmas cakes and iced fancies. He bent down to tie a shoelace and waste a little time. A familiar smell wafted from somewhere inside. Clouds of steam were billowing from an invisible back room. A sweating baker emerged from the mist, with a great pudding perched on a platter. He left it on a shelf to cool. Soon it would be added to the pile of puddings on the counter and sold for the Christmas celebrations.

Sam's mouth began to water as he recalled Christmases gone by. They were poor, but his mother saved a little money each week to give him a happy Christmas. He always felt snug and secure in their little house, seated in front of the log fire and gazing at the faces in the flames. Sometimes he would close his eyes and wish it could all go on for ever.

It was a dismal and bitter December morning; one of those dusky winter days when it never seems to get light. On the odd occasion he was sober his father had treated him to hot chestnuts at Greenwich market and now Sam detected a familiar odour. He turned and sure enough a chestnut seller was roasting nuts on a hot brazier by the kerb. A group of vagrants warmed themselves by the hot coals, while the vendor guarded his wares from their straying hands. Sam's mouth watered for a bag of hot nuts with blackened skins but Carrie had no money and in any case she was afraid of Jack finding out.

They left Oxford Street and entered a side road that Sam recognized and loved, for there stood a tiny shop stacked with toys. At this time of year it was especially full, and right at the front were his favourites, a drum and a small bugle. The jovial shopkeeper, a skilled patterer in a striped apron, stood in the doorway with a tin tray and demonstrated a clown that righted itself when pushed over.

The boy stopped, smiled and looked up at him, politely asking how much it cost. The man's manner changed at the sight of the young ragamuffin and Sam was urged to 'get lost' in low growling tones that had lost their jollity. The boy stayed just long enough to press his nose to the window and leave two small puffs of condensation, before the shopkeeper made towards him and Carrie hurried him on.

'You'll catch it if Jack hears you've been loitering. He doesn't trust you as it is,' his aunt said in a worried voice.

The routine for the robberies was the same as before, with Sam keeping watch, Ernie stealing the clothes and Carrie putting them in her basket. By the third house their lookout decided the weather was too cold for work and disappeared. So Ernie and Sam were left to climb a garden wall on their own.

The wall was a difficult one and Ernie's foot slipped at the top, causing him to plunge headfirst into the ditch below. At first he didn't move and Sam thought he was dead. The boy jumped down, pulled Ernie's head out of the water and dragged him clear. Ernie began to take shallow breaths but without recovering consciousness. His eyes were still closed and his face was covered in mud and dead leaves. Sam's heart skipped a beat. What if Ernie were dying?

'I think he's hurt bad, Aunty Carrie,' said Sam, 'there's a great big bump on his head. We ought to get him back to the house but I can't lift him over the wall.'

'I blame that great brute— he should 'ave been 'ere to 'elp 'im over, then all this wouldn't have happened,' said Carrie in a frightened voice. 'Just you wait till Jack 'ears about this, he'll kill me an' that scoundrel, I shouldn't wonder. There's nothing else for it, you'll have to go back to the 'ouse an' tell Jack.'

Sam ran down the alleyway. He felt elated and could have danced for joy. He was free at last, all he had to do was find a policeman and tell him everything. Then the gang would be arrested and he could go back to school. In the next street was the lookout, outside a low tavern, laughing and joking with friends as they drank beer together. His back was to Sam and the boy grew in confidence. Dodging the man would be easy and Sam slipped silently into a side street.

The boy looked down at his scruffy clothes. If he approached a policeman directly there could be problems. For one thing he could be taken as a vagrant and told not to waste police time. That was if he was listened to at all. Or he might get taken to his uncle's house, and because the Pineapple was a smooth talker, he might persuade the officer that there was no kidnap and Sam was only being mischievous.

No, there was nothing else for it. He would have to go to the lodging house in Kensington to tell Mrs Clayton and she could contact the police.

A crocodile of schoolgirls was walking on the other side of the street but apart from that the road was empty. The uniforms were quite unusual, Sam thought. There were many expensive schools for both girls and boys in London's West End, but these girls were wearing blue headscarves, something he had never seen before. The rest of the uniform consisted of a smart blue dress with a clean white collar and a blue apron.

Then it dawned on Sam, they were all carrying buckets in one hand and scrubbing brushes in the other. Steam was rising from warm water inside the buckets. They weren't a school at all but one of the step girls' brigades that Poll had spoken about.

What a fool he'd been; he must be half-asleep. The girl dawdling at the back, out of step with the others and in a dream, was Poll. He'd recognize her anywhere. The woman at the front of the crocodile was now detailing the girls to different doorsteps along the street; she must be the brigade leader.

Sam ran across the road. By now Poll was kneeling down and preparing to scrub a step. He tapped her on the shoulder.

'Poll, it's me Sam.' The girl turned and her eyes widened.

'Why, Sam, I thought I'd never see you again. But where have you been?' she said with a look of amazement that turned slowly into a smile. 'Tom and me looked everywhere but we couldn't find you. He feels really guilty because he said he'd look after you. Rob Roy's had the police out and they're still searching. Oh, Sam, all of us have been praying for you.'

Swiftly, Sam told Poll the whole story, from his separation from Tom outside the Crystal Palace to his kidnapping and imprisonment by his Uncle Jack, and finally his escape.

'I'm on my way to the Shoeblacks' Lodging now. I'm going to tell them everything,' said Sam. As he spoke a donkey cart turned into the street some way from where they stood.

'Don't go on your own, Sam,' said Poll, 'I'll leave this step and come with you.' She looked anxious. 'We don't want your uncle to catch us. If I saw 'im, I'd give 'im a piece of my mind, I can tell you.'

Sam looked up and abruptly shrank back into the doorway, all his confidence gone. He recognized both the donkey and the driver; it was Carrots with Pineapple Jack. Alfie sat by his side and they moved slowly past the houses, calling out for 'rags and old iron'. It was the one honest piece of business that Jack did. There wasn't a moment to lose, the doorway would not hide him for long. In a minute or so at the most Jack would see him, or if by some chance he didn't, then Carrots, who loved his friends even as he hated his enemies, would sniff him out.

'He's here Poll, he's here on the donkey cart,' said Sam, who was terrified of being recaptured. 'Don't look up for the moment and listen carefully to what I've got to say.'

78

Poll could tell from the tone of his voice that he was serious, so she did as she was told. 'He'll see me in a minute and I'll have to talk to him. He's the ugly one with the cap and the scarred face. While we're talking, look at him and remember his face. He'll want to see Ernie for himself. Then follow me but at a distance and keep going till I get back to Jack's house. Make sure you're not caught and then you can tell the police.'

Sam stepped out of the doorway and walked along the street. Boldness was the best policy. 'Hello, Uncle Jack, I've been looking for you. It's Ernie, he's hurt himself.' Jack looked up, surprised. Good, he hadn't seen him talking to Poll.

'Hurt, Ernie's hurt, who's hurt him?' said Jack reaching for his knife. He always liked to protect his investments. Sam saw Poll out of the corner of his eye and she stared at Jack for a long time. She was trying to memorize his face.

'No one hurt him. He fell from a garden wall and got knocked out. The lookout had disappeared, so Carrie sent me.' The lookout would be in serious trouble from Jack and a severe beating was the best he could expect. But if Sam had said nothing Carrie would get hurt. 'Do you want me to take you to him, Uncle Jack?'

'No, you just tell me, I knows the area. If you want a job doing, do it yourself, that's what I always say. No, you go back to the 'ouse with Alfie 'ere an' I'll take the cart.' Sam gave his uncle directions to the scene of the accident and Jack drove off muttering about lookout's duties.

Sam had no need to hold a conversation on the way back to the farmhouse, because Alfie did all the talking. He was proud of his skills both as pickpocket and footpad and he proceeded to tell the boy all about his adventures. Indeed, he was so pleased with himself that he failed to notice Sam turn his head and glance back from time to time. All the young shoe black had to do was to roar with laughter when his companion expected it, and Alfie revelled in the adulation.

Poll was very good at tailing them and Sam knew that even if Alfie turned round he would see nothing suspicious. She was just a young girl walking somewhere, unconnected with either of them. She kept about a hundred yards behind most of the time, and once, when they stopped at the kerb to allow a horse and carriage by, she ducked into a doorway.

In crowded Oxford Street, their progress was so slow she nearly caught them up but when Sam turned round, she was carefully examining ball gowns in a shop window. If he hadn't known her better, he'd have thought she was about to buy one.

The wasteland was a bit more difficult for the girl because there were few houses but she coped by keeping behind hedges and trees. Sam knew Poll could see them as they reached the farmhouse but to be on the safe side he left his cap on the gate post.

Once inside he was left alone, because there was no Jack to be suspicious and Teddy was still out. He looked out of the window and saw Poll carefully studying the house and then, quite suddenly, she was gone.

Sam felt his stomach tense with excitement but he was careful not to show it. It was best to act normally because the police would not come for some time. Poll had to reach the Uxbridge Road, cross Hyde Park and locate the Shoeblacks' Lodging house. Then she'd have to find Tom, who would take her to Mrs Clayton, who would inform the police. He prepared himself for a long wait.

About an hour later, Jack arrived on the donkey cart. Sam saw him carry a grinning Ernie into the house and place him carefully on to a pile of rags.

'Now you stay there son and look after yourself. We need lads like you to keep the business going,' said Jack. He turned to another boy. ''Ere you, fetch 'im some gin will yer?'

Aunty Carrie came in and Sam noticed fresh bruises on her face but she'd fared well compared to their lookout, who was covered in blood and could hardly walk. He staggered in and slumped, groaning under the stairs.

Carrie hurried out of Jack's sight while Sam stood and trembled. He couldn't leave Jack's house soon enough. The bushes moved in the garden of a ruined house across the road and Sam glimpsed a blue headscarf. It was Poll; she had obviously waited to make sure that this was where Jack lived. Clever girl, thought Sam and when he looked again the headscarf had gone.

That evening the drinking was heavy and Sam was glad, because he wanted the den of thieves to be ill prepared when the police came. Jack treated Ernie as the hero of the hour and even Sam came in for some praise.

'I tell yer, I was proud of the boy, 'e's only eight but 'e's like a soldier, injured in the line o' duty.' The bandaged Ernie gave a beaming smile and was unbearable for the rest of the evening.

'And my nevvy 'ere, young Sam, 'e came and told me what 'ad 'appened. I think we can trust 'im now, 'e don't 'ave to sleep in the little room no more. 'E can sleep along o' the rest o' yer. I wish we 'ad more like these two, to tell yer the troof,' continued Jack, glaring at Carrie and at the recumbent youth groaning under the stairs.

The drinking got heavier and heavier as the evening wore on but the police still did not come. Sam pretended to drink but always poured his away while no one was looking. By midnight most of the household were in a drunken stupor and he slept in a gap between snoring bodies. Sam lay fretting about Polly. Something must have happened. Then, at last, he dozed.

Sam awoke with a start. He glanced at the others; they were fast asleep, still under the influence of drink. He went to the window to estimate the time and noticed the sky becoming light, in the direction of Oxford Street. It was about dawn; quite late in the short days before Christmas. Then he saw a lantern flash in the half light and then another. He strained his eyes and could just make out the outlines of uniformed police officers. A cab drew up and a sergeant alighted. A sledgehammer was produced and Sam could see the sergeant giving orders.

The police had evidently decided that a night raid was too risky, because it gave experienced thieves a chance to slip away in the darkness. In the background Sam could see another cab with Rob

Roy and there, close by, were Polly and Tom. She had successfully guided Rob Roy and the police to the farmhouse.

The officer with the sledgehammer was advancing on the door with several others and Sam heard a splintering crash. The police were in and several occupants were arrested before they had properly wakened. People were running in all directions, shouting and screaming, and there was total chaos.

Polly and Tom looked at the prisoners being taken from the house and then moved closer, hoping to see Sam. Suddenly a middle-aged man with stubbly whiskers and wearing a cap, jumped from a window.

'It's him, Pineapple Jack!' shouted Polly and a policeman grabbed at him. But the man moved quickly, zig-zagging from side to side and eluding several officers. He would have got clear away but for Tom who pivoted as the man ran past. The boy threw his arms round the criminal's waist and slid down his body till the knees locked, bringing him crashing down. Sergeant Cobb, the officer in charge, was across in an instant, with a pair of handcuffs.

'So this is the great Pineapple Jack,' said the sergeant with heavy irony. The man started to recover.

'I'll have you know I'm not Pineapple Jack. I'm Mickey the Screever. You won't catch Jack neither, he's much too fly for you,' said Mickey in cultured tones.

'I'm sorry,' said Polly as they led the man away, 'I thought they was all boys, apart from Jack.' The sergeant gave her an encouraging smile.

'No need to worry. It's none too easy to see in the half light.' He turned to Tom. 'Thank you, son, you did well, you're a brave lad. Mr Macgregor will be pleased.'

Sam still had not appeared and Polly was worried. Tom suggested they look down the side of the house. The fence into the yard was broken and they wriggled through a gap.

'Look, over there, that must be the donkey's stable,' shouted Polly.

They ran across the yard and the door was swinging open. The fence at the back was down and driving away on the cart across the waste land, was Pineapple Jack holding tightly to Sam.

'Sergeant Cobb, he's got Sam!' yelled Tom, as the officer entered the yard. The sergeant quickly assessed the situation.

'He's headed for the Uxbridge Road, we can catch him in my cab. Do either of you know what Pineapple Jack looks like?' he said to Poll and Tom.

'Yes, I do,' said Polly.

'You can come with me. We might need you for identification. And you, you might come in useful,' he said to Tom. 'My men can follow in the other cab.'

As the two cabs set out, the sergeant and the children in the lead, they could just see the donkey cart turning into the Uxbridge Road.

Chapter 8
BLACKWALL ON THE THAMES

When the police burst in, Sam retreated to another room and hid beneath a pile of rags to avoid arrest. He planned to wait for his friends to enter and then come out. Unfortunately for Sam, Teddy, who had wanted revenge ever since Alfie's arrest, kept watch on him. So when Jack came downstairs, the young footpad pulled the rags to one side, revealing the hiding place.

'I mighta known it, it was you, yer little rat. You gave me away didn'tcha?' snarled the Pineapple. Sam noticed the two pistols in his belt. 'Pretty, ain't they?' he said, 'an' they're loaded too. I'm taking you with me, to make sure the esclop behave.'

'What about me, Jack? I'm yer mate, I 'elped yer, I told yer where Sam was,' wailed Teddy. A policeman burst in and Jack pushed Teddy viciously towards him. The boy reeled across the room, crashed into the officer and they fell in a struggling heap to the floor.

'You 'elped me again,' jeered Jack, as he tucked Sam under his arm and made good his escape into the yard. At the back of the stable was an old fence, which fell apart with one blow from Jack's boot. 'I knew that would 'appen, I've 'ad this planned for a long time,' said Jack. 'Only you can't trust no one in this game.' It was the work of a few moments to harness Carrots to the cart and they were away before anyone noticed.

It was a bumpy ride across the wasteland and the Pineapple tied Sam's arms with a crude noose of rope, which he fastened to a hook behind the driver's seat. This left his hands free to control the donkey and cart. As they approached the Uxbridge Road, Sam noticed two cabs leave the farmhouse and begin to follow.

Jack looked too, cursed under his breath and muttered something about 'givin' 'em the slip in the park'. They turned into Hyde Park and made for the Serpentine Bridge. As they crossed the famous lake and neared the Crystal Palace, the chasing cabs were passing through the gate. The police were gaining. Sam peered across at the great palace of glass and thought how lonely and sad it seemed, now the Great Exhibition was over.

On they went, out of the park on the south side, into the street, past the barracks, past the magnificent Apsley House, home of the Duke of Wellington, and along Piccadilly. Jack drove Carrots hard as he could, cursing and snarling the whole time and fingering the handle of a pistol. But the donkey cart was no match for horse-drawn cabs and their pursuers began to overtake them.

By the time they reached the Haymarket Sam could see Polly and Tom quite clearly and there was a distance of perhaps six carriage lengths between them. By now the morning traffic was heavy and it came to Jack's aid. The donkey cart was light and manoeuvrable, so Jack was able to dodge about among the vehicles and maintain his lead.

They passed through Trafalgar Square and in the Strand the cabs gained ground once more. Jack looked desperate and Sam wondered what he would do. The boy was just beginning to feel pleased at the thought of rescue, when the Pineapple turned sharp left into Covent Garden, the great fruit market.

The move was unexpected but typical of Jack's cunning. Its success was insured when the progress of the police vehicles was prevented by a massive brewer's waggon with two huge horses. It had stopped in their path because of heavy traffic. Sergeant Cobb was furious. He jumped down and shouted at the driver, who edged resentfully forwards.

But it was too late. When they got to the market, they stopped in dismay. There were donkey carts as far as the eye could see, most being loaded with fruit and vegetables. Finding one among so many was simply impossible.

Sergeant Cobb was bitterly disappointed. Pineapple Jack had been a menace for a long time and the sergeant badly wanted to capture him. But now the man had slipped away in the streets of London and the chance had gone.

The sergeant twiddled the end of his moustache nervously. He could feel himself starting to sweat. 'Can either of you children think where Jack might have gone?' he asked with quiet desperation in his voice. Tom racked his brains.

'Well, he came from Greenwich and he knows lots of people there, and one of them might give him a hiding place,' said Tom.

'You might be right. At any rate, it's our only chance. He'll have to cross the river, so we'll try London Bridge. That's the most direct route to Greenwich,' said the sergeant and they set off at a gallop for the Thames.

Sergeant Cobb drove hard and within minutes they were in Upper Thames Street, a narrow cobbled road running parallel to the Thames. There was no sign of the Pineapple anywhere.

'London Bridge is the next turning on the right but we seem to have missed them,' said the sergeant slowing down and anxiously scanning the street. 'Perhaps they went another way.' Just then a donkey cart crossed the road ahead of them and made for the bridge.

'It's him and Sam's with him!' shouted Poll, and the sergeant increased speed. Jack was now held up in a traffic queue on the approach to the bridge and he was completely trapped as the cab drove straight at him.

Tom really thought they had him at last but Jack was desperate.

The vehicles were about to collide when he pulled out a pistol and fired directly at his pursuers. The cab swerved wildly to one side as Sergeant Cobb jerked the rein and they mounted the pavement. A sliver of wood flew out from a beam above an ancient shop front. The pistol ball screamed as it ricocheted away into the distance. The shot was way off target but it had done its job. Jack was once more making away at high speed and the cab was slewed across the pavement.

After hurling a torrent of abuse at the police and flinging his empty pistol at them, he turned the cart across the traffic, abandoned London Bridge and headed for the City. A few minutes were lost as the sergeant, not without difficulty, managed to get the cab back on the road. Then a wild chase ensued in which Jack risked his own life, as well as Sam's, in an attempt to avoid capture. He veered recklessly from one side of the road to the other and when forced to corner he went round on one wheel.

Sam looked nervously at his uncle's face but there was no recognition, just a mad, haunted stare. He had missed the way to Greenwich, where his booty was stashed and there was now no way of getting there. It could only be a matter of time before the police caught up with him.

They left the City, with the Tower on the right and entered the Highway. Sam saw the tops of ships' masts looming above the high walls of St Katherine's Dock; they were coming to the docklands area.

The shops changed their nature and took on a nautical flavour. Many were ships' chandlers with anchors, ropes, knives, compasses and chronometers on display. Others sold special clothing for the sailors. Crews from docked ships thronged everywhere, some in naval uniform and others in exotic garments, spilling out from the local taverns on to the streets.

Then more ships' masts, this time in the London Docks and soon they were in the village of Limehouse. Suddenly the cart began to shake. Carrots was exhausted and beginning to stumble, the chase was almost over. Sam heard Jack mutter something that sounded like 'West India Dock'.

The cart cornered so fast that it was on one wheel for several seconds and Sam would have fallen into the road but for the bonds that held him. He looked back and the police cabs were closing fast.

Out of the corner of his eye he spied a well-dressed lady and gentleman emerging from a greengrocer's shop. They seemed somehow familiar but Sam couldn't quite place them. Then he got it. He had cleaned the man's boots. It was Lieutenant Hopwood from the Great Exhibition, this time not in uniform. The lieutenant was looking at him in amazement and Sam seized the opportunity to shout for help.

'Lieutenant Hopwood, it's me, Sam. I'm a prisoner!' the boy screamed and the soldier turned to follow. The donkey cart sped past a startled gatekeeper and close behind were the police, followed by Lieutenant Hopwood sprinting like a champion.

Right inside was a dock and Carrots stopped dead by the quayside, then flatly refused to go another step. Sam wasn't surprised; he looked fatigued and clouds of steam were rising from his flanks. Jack unhitched Sam, keeping his arms tied and laid him on the ground. Then he pulled out his second pistol but only just in time, because Sergeant Cobb was almost on top of him.

'Don't you come no nearer or the whelp gets it,' roared Jack and the sergeant slowly backed off. Sam seized his chance. While the Pineapple's attention was on the policeman the boy rolled to one side and was several yards away before Jack noticed. Even then he might have caught the boy but for Lieutenant Hopwood.

He advanced towards Jack in such a determined manner that the gang leader was visibly worried. He pointed the pistol at the soldier who ignored it and walked on. The assembled pursuers simply stood and stared, not knowing what to do for the best.

Sam heard the sound of a ship's siren and a paddle steamer entered the dock. Still the soldier advanced. A look of panic appeared on Jack's face and the pistol began to shake. The old confidence had gone and when he did fire, the ball whistled harmlessly over his opponent's shoulder. Then the two were grappling for a hold.

For several seconds they stood straining, with their arms clasped around each other and then slowly Jack was forced on to his toes. The steamer was closer now and Sam saw the name, one he had seen before – Leith, Edinburgh to London. A pipe band in military tunics and kilts was entertaining the passengers. Suddenly Lieutenant Hopwood bent at the knees, turned his hip and Pineapple Jack catapulted through the air, hitting the paving slabs with a ground-shaking thud.

His head cracked back and the breath was audibly forced out of his body. He lay unconscious, while the soldier turned and asked the sergeant for handcuffs. Sergeant Cobb reached into his pocket and after rummaging desperately, eventually produced a pair.

'Watch out, it's Jack!' shouted Tom. The seemingly impossible had happened, Jack had dragged himself to his feet and was staggering drunkenly towards the dock. The pipe band stopped playing and Sam saw the astonished stares of the pilot and helmsman. They all watched helplessly, those on board as well as those on shore, as he reached the quayside, tottered for a second and then pitched forward into the water. Moments later a giant paddle wheel struck him and he disappeared from view.

The breathless watchers examined the churning waters for signs of life but there was nothing. Then perhaps twenty yards away, a peaked cap with sequins bobbed up, turned over and sank, never to be seen again.

'There was nothing we could do. You can't stop a ship that size in just a few feet,' said the captain, visibly shaken. The Leith had docked, and the captain, pilot and helmsman had come back to see what had caused the accident.

'No need to worry. We don't blame you,' said Sergeant Cobb. 'He is, or should I say, was a notorious criminal we've been after for a long time. This time he was engaged in kidnapping the young boy over there.' The sergeant indicated Sam, now released from his bonds and recovering from his ordeal.

Mrs Hopwood seemed very concerned about Sam and she

examined him carefully for bruises and rope burns. 'Sam appears well,' she said to her husband, 'there's nothing broken but he feels very shaken.' She paused for a moment as a thought struck her. 'How silly of me. I'd quite forgotten about the donkey. Poor thing, he must be exhausted after that long ride. Shall I feed him, Sam?'

Before Sam could speak she walked across to a Carrots now fully recovered and contentedly grazing on a stretch of grass, by a wooden hoist tower, one of the many used for loading and unloading freight. Mrs Hopwood opened her string bag and offered the animal a turnip. Sam tried to yell but it was too late. Carrots was baring his teeth and pawing the ground with his hind leg, in an alarming manner. It's the wrong shape, the wrong colour and the wrong smell, thought Carrots. I'm not that tired and I'm not standing for it. It took Sam several minutes of soothing words, together with petting and stroking to calm him down.

* * * *

Sam woke with a start and tried to recall where he was. Then he remembered; he was in his little bedroom, with its oak beams, in his new home in the pretty riverside village of Blackwall. It was still dark on a February morning in 1852, two months after his crazy ride through London with Pineapple Jack. Possibly he had been awakened by some noise or other from one of boats that passed their riverside house. He wasn't sure but he didn't mind anyway; he had grown up with the traffic on the Thames and he found the sounds comforting.

Soon after his rescue, Sam had been adopted by Richard and Charlotte Hopwood. It was something the lieutenant had wanted months earlier, after they met at the Great Exhibition. But when they returned to tell him, they learnt from Tom he had been kidnapped and had disappeared for ever. The Hopwoods resigned themselves to never seeing him again and were overjoyed to have the chance to help free him. 'Who says that prayers are never answered?' smiled Sam to himself. 'All the time that I doubted God, he had the perfect parents already lined up for me.'

Sam smiled as he thought of the trip to the toyshop near Oxford Street on Christmas Eve, the day he moved in at Blackwall. Mrs Hopwood had bought him new clothes, then taken him shopping for presents. The shopkeeper failed to recognize the former ragged urchin and even gave a little bow, as if he were serving the son of a lord. Sam rolled over in bed to make sure they were still there, the bugle and the drum, and he smiled to see them right at the top of his toybox.

Then he remembered why he had wakened early; it was the day of his birthday party. He had never had a party before and all his friends, both old and new, were coming. Children from his new school at the nearby St Matthias Church would be along and so would Tom and Polly. Sam loved the interior of the ancient church with its pillars made from the wooden masts of sailing ships belonging to the East India Company. In fact the church was used as the Chapel of the East India Company. He got up, washed, dressed and went downstairs to find his new father sitting in an armchair reading *The Times*.

'Good morning, Sam,' he said, 'I've got an extra present for you.' He tossed what looked like a book to the boy.

'What is it, Papa?' said Sam, looking puzzled.

'Try and read it, Sam. It's a bit difficult but I'll help you,' said his father.

'Catalogue of the Great Exhibition of the Works and Industry of all Nations,' read Sam, with a great deal of prompting from his father.

'I got it as a souvenir for you, something to look back on when you grow up. It didn't cost me anything. They're giving them away now. The Crystal Palace is completely empty and they've taken out all the exhibits. It seems strange now, so quiet after all that activity. They're talking about moving it to south London, Croydon or Norwood, somewhere like that. Apparently, the horseback riders of

Hyde Park are complaining that it's been built right across the riding paths,' continued Lieutenant Hopwood.

Sam thought how loving and helpful his father was— something that took a bit of getting used to after living with the treachery of Pineapple Jack. His former life had all seemed so real at the time but now it was all like a dream, although he did worry from time to time that Jack's body had never been found. Supposing he were still alive?

Lieutenant Hopwood had been to the Registrar's Office soon after they had adopted Sam and obtained a birth certificate for him. It turned out that the boy had been eleven in November, three months ago, and today had been chosen as his official birthday so he wouldn't miss out.

'You'll have two birthdays this year, to make up for having none last year,' his new mother joked.

Sam's father was speaking again. 'I was talking to Mr Macgregor and he's going to open up more shoeblack brigades. The one you belonged to, the original one, is to be called The Central London Reds and guess what, Tom is in charge of them. Macgregor was very impressed by his showing such bravery on two occasions in combating Jack's gang, and, in any case, the boy is a born leader. This is his big chance in life.'

'It's just what I've been praying about all these months!' shouted Sam with delight, jumping up and down on the spot with excitement.

Lieutenant Hopwood smiled. 'It's wonderful news that your prayers have been answered, Sam. And you'll be pleased to learn that your mother and I chose your new school carefully to help you discover more about the works of God. The headmaster is a good friend of our family and a faithful Christian gentleman.'

'By the way, they're redecorating up at Field Lane and when I dropped in to make a donation, Mr White gave me these.' Lieutenant Hopwood held up the notices that Sam had so wanted to read but hadn't been able to.

Sam smiled and read them smoothly, without a pause. 'Thou shalt not kill; Thou shalt not steal; Thou shalt not bear false witness; The Lord is my shepherd. It's easy when you know how!' shouted Sam, laughing and clapping his hands.

After the party Sam continued to live happily with his new parents. Tom left the lodging, went back home to live and really did earn enough, as a chargehand in the shoeblacks, for his own keep and schooling for his brothers and sister.

Mrs Hopwood found a sempstress, at nearby Mile End, who was prepared to allow Polly to lodge with her and teach her how to sew. Her dancing days were over. Another of Sam's prayers was answered when Lieutenant Hopwood managed to locate her sister, Mary, who had gone to a ragged school in Southwark after running away. The two girls shared the lodging until they were old enough to look after themselves.

Sam attended the trial of those arrested at Jack's house. At first the magistrate had wanted to transport them all to Australia but Rob Roy pleaded on behalf of the boys. Most of them were let off provided they attended ragged schools and learnt a trade. Sam was very glad for Ernie, who at eight was too young to be branded a criminal.

The old woman, who did the cleaning at the Shoeblacks' Lodging, had died. The Claytons needed somebody and Mr Macgregor suggested Aunty Carrie. The magistrate agreed, although she was bound over to keep the peace. Mickey the Screever and his wife Sal were unfit for trial and they were both confined to the debtors' part of Newgate Prison where they died within a year.

In the end only Teddy and his brother, Alfie, were transported. The magistrate wasn't prepared to send them to school, on account of the extreme violence of their attacks on the public.

As for Carrots, he came to live with the Hopwoods in a stable at the back of the house. He was loved by everyone he took a liking to, and eventually he forgave even Mrs Hopwood, although he became very fretful whenever he caught sight of her string bag. In the end she was forced to get rid of it and buy a cloth one instead. After that they became firm friends and remained so, right to the end of his long life.

Blackwall is situated on the eastern side of the great tonsil-shaped bend of the Thames that contains the Isle of Dogs.

Sometimes, after the Sunday morning service at St Matthias, the family would take a ride on the donkey cart down past the new West India Docks. After that they were in open country.

Sam loved the flat fields of Millwall, with its many windmills that stood out like giants marching across the sky. He felt the wind from the Thames blowing through his hair as Carrots trotted down to the southern tip of the Island. From there he could see Greenwich, his old home and also feel secure in his new family. He couldn't complain, life had been tough at times but God was good and now the future was bright.